Split-Tales
Of
Split-Tails

Split-Tales Of Split-Tails

Pat Parsons

Library of Congress Control Number: 2021903589

HARDBACK: 978-1-955347-27-3
PAPERBACK: 978-1-955347-26-6
EBOOK: 978-1-955347-28-0

Ordering Information:

For orders and inquiries, please contact:
1-888-404-1388
www.goldtouchpress.com
book.orders@goldtouchpress.com

Printed in the United States of America

Contents

SPLIT TALES SPLIT TAILS
OF
Here's The Author
"PAT PARSONS"
with his
Very Relaxing And Peaceful
Introduction With Poetry Appreciation
For Dreamy thoughts!!!

Introduction

This book is a depicture in the life of a young man and the many many pleasurable events that he made sure took place in the time allotted to him by "God's" great gift of life.

Even as a young child he made it a priority to enjoy every second of every happening. Whether they be good or bad never became the decision-maker as to how long an event would last. Especially if it were something he had experienced before.

One thing he had learned and became very familiar with at quite a young age was, if given the time and attention, something bad could be turned into something good. At a very young age his mindset was, bad is not fun. Knowing he was born for fun, in his younger years he spent a lot of time turning bad into good. Eventually with "God's" help, he got it all under control.

He was able to live a life that most people could only dream about. Knowing one day he would be granted the opportunity to enlighten others on the importance of living a life of happiness, he took notes and made tapes of different situations and conversations about events that took place in his wonderful life.

By drawing from his world of afterglow and with the help of his memoirs, he has been able to relive a fresh lifetime of exposure. Conveying sometimes blow-by-blow descriptions of the actual events of his life. By doing so he provided a tantalizer to interest that created the desire for continued reading.

As you are taking your, sometimes shockingly unusual, literary journey through the tangled tales as they unravel and form the life of this young man. One would be well advised to keep an open mind, while remembering, silence is no friend to a writers pen. I try hard to put into perspective that I am reading the evolution of his subjectivity. I believe the majority of people can agree, the direction our lives will take is determined by what we are taught or introduced to through our younger years. Some of us are encouraged to start learning earlier in life than others. Such as the young man whose life is being portrayed in this book.

The undying desire he possessed to satisfy by making each and every one of his partners happy, he has extended to you through his literary genius. As you are traveling through time turning the pages of his life. You should not be surprised if it seems as though you are the author and you are writing your life. Through the terminology and proper placing of events with fruitful description that openly demands partaking. You might sometimes have no choice except to find yourself in his place and be happy to be there.

For many many years it has been determined there are seven wonders of the world. To this author there have always been eight. The eighth wonder can be that of natural resources. This would categorize it as being a natural wonder. The eighth wonder could also be that of man-made source and categorized as a man-made wonder. But in the heart, mind, body, and soul of this author, the eighth wonder of the world can only be accomplished through a combination of both natural and man-made desires and resources. This author's interpretation of the eighth wonder of the world would be and always has been, the culmination of the ultimate satisfaction to any and all acts in the art of making love. Then and only then, can it be considered an event worthy of "**WONDER**" status!!!

<u>"POEMS of APPRECIATION"</u>

each one of them are so very important to me
and have a special place in my heart,
I think of them often and drink to them always
knowing we shall never part;
from the grassy mounds I explored as a child
to the Red Snapper I was taught to devour,
from the fishy freshwater skinny-dipping trips
to the homecoming queen as the lady of the hour;
from my beautifully bountiful days of bondage
living with lust on my lips for their love so soft,
feeling my way through that fabulous frontline of Southern Bells
while teaching me how to keep their clothes off:
"As I open my arms and my heart to those I hold
tight but tenderly in my world of afterglow,
I love them all, I miss them all and now I know
they all know our love lives on in afterglow;
they take their place and with all their charm
cannot help but overflow,
with their proudly possessed worthiness they fill
my world of afterglow;
my eyes are tempted with tepid tears,
to warm the memories from our tender times of yesteryear;
I thank you all so very much for the part you played then
and the part you are playing now in my world,
so strange I guess it seems to some that I can say now
to all of you, that you will always be my girls!!!"

Dedication

The book itself is dedicated to all the young ladies that allowed my pursuit for happiness to be achieved. They allowed me to live a full and complete life while experiencing the wonders of love. I have nothing but love and appreciation for each and every one of them and I treasure the pleasure of holding them in my heart forever.

The book's title is dedicated to one of my favorite aunts. She was famous for her verbal delivery of colorfully insulting name-calling when referring to almost anyone in our hometown. The term split-tails was one of those nicknames she used for young ladies pursuing any of her sons. She even sometimes cursed the ground they walked on as well as the beds they slept in.

I however, ask "God" to bless the ground they walked on. And I thanked "God" every day for them and the beds they slept in. Especially if I were fortunate enough for it to have been my bed.

These wonderfully beautiful and abundantly gracious young ladies are certainly deserving of any and all the respect and thankfulness I can verbally display or mentally imagine. They provided me with everything I needed to accomplish the most important thing I could ever do in life.

I was possessed with getting to them before they got to me. I somehow had to make sure they were more satisfied and much happier when we parted than they were when we met.

Chapter 1
"Pussy Packing"

My story began when I was quite young and became the recipient of the worst ass-beating anybody ever had. I had been playing with my little next-door neighbor girl-friend. The exploratory process quite naturally for me came into play. It seemed no matter how hard I tried I was unable to complete the process of fitting our body parts together. For some strange reason, I got this overwhelmingly un-dismissible desire to pack the little split-open-hole between her legs full of something. That little split-open-hole later became known to me as a pussy.

My older brother and sister and her older brother and sister were sitting on the back porch swing when I came out of the building we were playing in. The only thing on my mind was finding something I could push into that little split-open-hole. I pulled a handful of grass then went immediately back inside the little building and took care of business.

Little did I know at the time that I was about to try to close the door on an entrance of one of the most popular reception parlors "God" ever created. All-powerful or overpowering might best describe this particular female orifice, being blessed with the power to tumble empires and bring the leaders to their knees. Large businesses, small businesses, important men, and even the average Joe - they are all pale in comparison to the power of the pussy.

Other words that come to mind are magnetic, addictive, controlling, time-consuming, delectable, delightful, deliriously delicious, and dynamically demanding. That pussy, that little split-open-hole, is only pale in power to its creator.

What was I thinking? I knew the very second I started pushing grass into her pussy my punishment was under-way. I could feel its fire burning my fingers as I tried to tenderly tuck away the tell-tale blades of grass. It seems they had already been charged with the duties of determining the upcoming soreness of my ass.

When my little friend went home, her mother saw all the tiny blades of grass, that were trying to free themselves from her panties. Needless to say, her mother met with my mother and my mother met me and my ass with a wet hand. Every time the water would splash off her hand when it came in contact with my ass, she would wet it again and smack it dry.

This punishment continued much too long as far as I was concerned. I made up my mind that I would be much more secretive while playing with a little girl's body parts.

I couldn't even have lied out of that if I had tried. There were too many witnesses. They voluntarily verified I had come out of the little building where we were playing and pulled a handful of grass. I'm sure they did it so they could laugh while my mother was playing the Star-Spangled-Banner on my ass.

Secrecy and doing a better job of picking and choosing places to play with little pussy was number one on my mind from that day forward. I think I must have played with every little pussy in my neighborhood over the next two or three years without suffering any type of punishment for my pussy playing pleasures.

I was a few years older before my next date with punishment. I got my face slapped for having my picture taken with another neighborhood girlfriend. I had my arm around her neck and draped over her shoulder allowing my hand to completely cover and compress her right titty. My mother was not happy and she let me know it.

There was always just something in the back of my mind about being caught. But there was also something very magnetic about that little split-open-hole between their legs that demanded my attention. I had this driving desire to try different things that could add to the excitement of my game playing efforts. I knew I must keep it a secret from my mother and I did just that. Hell, I had already experienced **the taste of honey from the well** and she never found out. One of my older playmates had taught me the cunt-licking process. It almost immediately became my number one goal to achieve perfection at the art of cunt-licking. I guess my addiction was developing at a faster pace or a younger age than most, and that was fine with me.

Chapter 2
"The Red Snapper"

My mother was working and felt she needed to hire somebody to watch me, like a babysitter I guess. She was the daughter of one of my mother's good friends. My mother had no problem letting her be my babysitter. After all, in those days, who would have expected a babysitter to go astray?

She was about four years older than I and her name was Jean. Jean also had kind of a waywardly, wondering mind. Over the next two or three years, we got to know each other very well.

Jean taught me a lot about all the things I really wanted to know. Things like how to make this work, where things go, and what happens when they get there. We had a lot of fun, and I enjoyed the time she spent as my babysitter/sex instructor.

Later in life from my memoirs, I wrote a poem about her. Actually, it was a song. Here are a few of the lines from that song: *"I had a babysitter, she was a real hand clapper, I used to sit on her knee, while she played with me, and showed me her red snapper."* By the time I was a couple of years older, I had become quite knowledgeable and was aware that Jeans RED-SNAPPER and the SPLIT-OPEN-HOLE between her legs were one. The same pleasures were provided by both. To award true definition was dependent on the declarer's state of mind at the time.

There was very little we had not experimented with, including foreign objects like vegetables and hot-dogs. Little did I know that the very necessary and enlightening time we spent together would play such an immensely important part in preparing me for all the good times I had to look forward to.

Chapter 3
"Snapper separation"

I didn't know exactly what caused it, but suddenly I had been sent off to a private Christian school. I was really happy to find out it was a co-ed school. Jean had spoiled me so much. I'm not sure what would have happened if it had not been co-ed.

Through some of the whispering conversations, I got tidbits of information that led me to believe my mother, Jean's mother, and my aunt thought we should be separated. And so it happened, what an unhappy day, no more sex training from Jean.

Thanks to the many things about sex and the female anatomy I had learned from Jean, the two years I spent in that particular private school were very productive and quite rewarding. All through school, especially my junior and senior Years when I was transferred back to my local high school, I was able to practice and became quite skilled in acquiring, performing for, and satisfying my sexual partners. All of which could be attributed to my favorite baby-sitter and her cute little RED-SNAPPER.

Jean's training became so helpful to me when it came to highlighting the obvious and accentuating just how glamorous life can be when love is in full bloom and our minds are free.

It had become very clear to me that I needed the company of either the same or a different young lady every day. Jean had certainly left her mark on me and put a dent in my heart as well. The demand in my mind for a daily discharge of bodily fluids was so overwhelming, and if not provided by a young lady, I would improvise. That was certainly not my favorite way to go, and as a result, I was in what you might call **hot pursuit** all the time.

I recall a comment made by one of my aunts during my senior year in high school. She told me I would be damn lucky if I lived to be 20 years old if I didn't stop chasing those **split-tails** around **(Hence the title of my book).** She also said, "Nothing good will ever come from it. They will either take your love or your money and maybe both. And they will leave when they are done with you. You will end up with a broken heart, a broken mind, and a broken bank account. You will have a lot of time to think about the wasted time." I didn't give it too much thought. Maybe I should have, after all, she was a **split-tail** and they say it takes one to know one. To say nothing of the fact that she was right about almost everything except the broken heart and broken mind parts. Instead, those wonderfully gorgeous and loving **SPLIT-TAILS** knew exactly what I wanted and needed to be happy.

They have rewarded me with more than much happiness and beautiful memories for my dreams of *afterglow*.

She was one of my favorite aunts, if not my favorite. She was always kind of funny and loved to add a little flavor to her comments. For example, the way she referred to young ladies as split-tails. That caused them to seem so much more appealing to me than they already were.

Their **split-tails** was the keeper of my key to happiness. It possessed a very strong magnetic force that sometimes seemed to just reach out grab me and pull me to it. So strong I had no other choice except to become a prisoner of **pussy.** I was totally in love with those three five-letter words that had favored me so much by flavoring my destiny.

Forever in search of a split-tail or two, or three, I knew as long as I could keep counting the number of split-tails, it would keep mounting. A little later in life, I was blessed with the honor of performing a **JOINT – EFFORT** with (5) wonderfully appreciative and playfully experimental **SPLIT-TAILS** on two king-size beds pushed together. I knew from the very beginning my goose was cooked. But I gave it my best-shot and had a lot of fun making that lasting loving memory in an apartment on Scott Circle in Washington, DC.

The year was 1965. What a great time it was to be involved in the sensual exploratory process of sex with five lively and luscious LAPS- of-LESBIAN-LOVERS!!!

•••

(Oh well, another book entry.)
don't miss it

•••

Chapter 4
"It's Party Time"

It was my 18th birthday and I was sitting in the study hall waiting for my turn to be called to the principal's office. He had put a program in place that made it seem like you were getting a birthday present if they had received feedback on job placement for you. If so, he would call your name over the PA system and wish you a happy birthday. Then he would request that you come to his office as soon as possible; he would like to have a few words with you.

I had already been informed by my uncle about the details of my job placement. I still wanted to go through the motions to show my appreciation to the principal for his help in securing that position for me. Although I had no intention of accepting that job offer, I felt it best to keep that decision to myself.

Graduation was just around the corner, as a matter-of-fact, it was only four days away. Wow, I was 18, which made me legally my own boss. I was graduating, those two events, in my mind, made me free to do and be whatever I felt like.

I was just kind of sitting there looking out the window going through my regular daydreaming mode. Suddenly, my name came over the PA system informing me that I should report the office.

When I got to the office, I was expecting to be greeted by the principal, however, I was met by our class president. Her name was Annette. She told me the principal had to go on an appointment and she was taking over his job placement responsibilities. Annette already knew that I had no desire to take the job I had been offered. We had discussed it a couple of days prior when she and a couple of other young ladies and I were at the library. I really wasn't sure why she had called me to the office, unless she was just going through the motions also.

We talked casually for a couple of minutes, then she reached into her purse, pulled out an envelope, and said to me, "Larry, I have to get back to work. I still have several students to call on, oh, by-the-way, happy birthday." She handed me the Envelope, then added, "Please make sure you let me know ASAP how you feel about this. I'd like to know by tomorrow so I can make plans." I took the envelope and told her, "Thank you very much, Annette. I don't know what it is I'm letting you know but I shall let you know it tomorrow. I'll come by your house. I don't like phones; there are too many people on party lines." She nodded okay and told me to make it after 2 PM.

I could've gone home, but I wanted to hang around the school as much as I could. That's where the girls were. I could go home anytime but the school would be over in just a few days.

There were a few sophomores and juniors that got my attention and I wanted to have the opportunity to wish them a very happy and fun-filled summer. The idea was to make as many connections as I could before summer vacation started. I wanted to be able to make the most of every pleasuring opportunity as it presented itself to me.

I went back to the study hall and sat down. I opened the envelope Annette had given me. It turned out to be a birthday card and an invitation to what sounded like a swimming party.

I was a little confused because I thought Annette was going steady with someone. But then I remembered I hadn't noticed her wearing a ring around her neck, since that was the thing back then I always checked it out. Availability was a priority on my checklist.

Before I had the opportunity to think anymore about it, I was greeted by two of my former playmates. Their names were Julia and Yvonne.

When I was quite young, the three of us enjoyed each other as often as possible. So much so they were both responsible for some of my worst punishment. I got my ass beat really bad over Yvonne and my face slapped a couple times because of Julia. Once I figured out how to keep from getting caught, we explored the healing powers of salt many times. We played the parts of inspired young doctors and nurses.

Since I returned from the private school I was sent to, the three of us have managed to get together several times. We pleasured each other with private swimming and deep-river-skinny-dipping-diving lessons. Julia and Yvonne made learning to provide and receive underwater lovemaking pleasures very exciting and sometimes interestingly dangerous.

I especially liked watching the two of them damn near drown while providing those pleasures to each other. There were a couple of times they provided me with a hard-on and a hand-job so I could feed the fish. Underwater hand-jobs can sometimes last forever without busting a nut. The fish have all the time they need to call their friends and family in for feasting. It can sometimes be a little scary.

Should you entertain the idea of having underwater sex, hand-jobs, finger-fucking, and regular sex is the safest way to go. You can keep your head above water and easily breathe. Performing an underwater (69'er) is not only excitingly challenging and healthy but can be very dangerous. Eating pussy underwater is a very good full-body exercise. If one can overcome the resistance provided by the under-current and maintain mouth to pussy connection, one might be able to increase one's lung capacity. If one could possibly get enough practice it might become a plus factor in the breath-holding process required for this particular act of sex.

One can also easily get mentally carried away. Knowing one is devouring this scrumptious piece of female flesh might entice the ignoring of one's underwater presence. If one tries to breathe to keep up the pace it could be dangerous, may be deadly. My advice is simply this: one should only attempt eating pussy underwater if **one's mouth and mind are in the right place!!!** And, of course, if one does not have heart trouble **(AW HELL, DO IT ANYWAY, IT"S FUN!!!).**

Whether it be freshwater or the ocean's saltwater, more pleasure is provided to the art of underwater pussy eating from the changes in flavor due to being submerged. The secretion flavors are totally different and they present a much more enticing burst of intimacy that screams for attention. It possesses the magnetic power and warm lustful lure of a pussy flavored to perfection and positively edible. Then it becomes more so and changes with the temperature of each arriving current or undertow. Being fully aware of the danger also places the demand for perseverance to consume and makes drowning easier. The givers of underwater blow-jobs, I would imagine are faced with similar circumstances. However, the recipient of such can enjoy the pleasures for a much longer period of time.

The three of us coming together in a lust-filled slushy underwater love-fest-fuck brought orgasms after orgasms because of the intriguing demands of delightful-danger.

Freshwater fucking is a lot of fun and very much underrated. Freshwater fucking equips one with stages of serendipity. It can also provide very unusually exciting serendipitous moments.

With the two of them, it was all about togetherness. It could never be one without the other. They were like peaches and cream, ice cream and cake, or even peanut butter and jelly. However, you wish to describe them, they were always together and very temptingly tasty. Together, we playfully explored the boundaries of menage a trois. In fact, we did so much exploring over those few years we became very proficient in knowing **where, when, and what to do so that we could all enjoy total satisfaction together.**

Most of the school seats back then were fold-up seats with the desk in front and a place to put books underneath. The seat was a little longer than necessary for the normal-sized student. Yvonne sat on the left edge and Julia squeezed in on the right edge facing me. They both leaned in towards me a little and began singing happy birthday. While doing so they were both running their fingers through my hair and massaging my shoulders. The study hall teacher was our class sponsor and she let it continue until it started to create a disturbance. Then she quietly approached my seat and told us we were just having too much fun for school. She said, "Happy birthday, Larry. You are all seniors and do you know you don't have to be here? School is technically over for you. So before you all get too carried away, why don't you girls find a place outside under a tree where it's nice and quiet to continue serenading Larry." And so it happened.

I always liked that teacher. She was my favorite teacher. She was my English teacher and was always commenting on how much she enjoyed reading my poetry. I would've liked to have taken her for a private poetry recital walk through the park. Teachers need love too and she had a very sexy esophagus that I would have just loved to travel. **The "E" Train** was born. Interpret that however you wish!!!

On the way outside, we stopped by my locker. I always kept a little something there to increase the intensity of the moment. One might refer to it as pick-em up poison, namely MOON_SHINE!!!

My locker was at the end of the hall. I could see the entire hallway. It was between classes and there was no-one around, which meant it was a perfect time for another one of our games, **"locker-soccer."**

The lockers were full-length lockers and provided pretty good body coverage. Having been there before and played this game, they both had their special places to be. Yvonne's favorite place to start was standing facing me. She was mostly hidden by the locker door, which I was holding in place for her cover. My back was to the wall so I had a full view of the hall and Julia fit perfectly in the locker.

The nearest classroom door was probably 30 or 40 feet away and it opened to feed the opposite direction. I had been able to perform this service several times and never been caught so I wasn't really worried about it. Besides, we were all seniors; what the hell were they going to do, kick us out of school?

Everybody's hands and mouths started finding places to go and things to do. I was holding the top of the door with my left hand to keep it in place to hide Yvonne. She had dropped to her knees, unzipped my jeans was jerk-sucking my cock.

Neither one of them were wearing bras. I think they had planned it that way knowing something crazy was going to happen for my birthday. I moved in and began massaging Julia's tits and nipples. I leaned in a little farther and gave her a kiss. Her lips immediately went after my tongue. We had eliminated being tongue shy almost at the beginning of our play days. I found out a long time ago that both these split-tails loved to suck tongue. They would suck anything that would fit in their mouth from a lollipop to a toe.

Yvonne was semi-soft-jerking me with her left hand while vacuum sucking the head of my prick. I felt it was time to give Julia a little finger fun. I guess they didn't think they needed panties either. Everything had been planned for easy access. Hell, I was probably the hardest one to get to.

I kinda needed a little helping hand so I tapped Yvonne on her right shoulder and pulled her arm up a little. She knew right away what I needed and she liked it. I believe she was a part boy. Her hand went immediately to Julia's cunt. I was sucking Julia's tits and grabbed Yvonne's right hand to pull her fingers out of Julia's pussy. I brought them to my lips and licked off the excess juices then returned them to gather more love lava. Then I delivered a soft, slow, and sloppy, secretion kiss to Julia's lips. We tongue wrestled for a few short seconds and laid claim to the last sample drops of her pussy's taste-tested generous juices.

Yvonne was working too hard. She was supplying a slow jerk on my shaft and hard suck to my pricks head and at the same time supplying Julia with a double-finger-fuck. I was trying to keep Julia happy but I was failing terribly. I realized all I could do was make promises for later and that's what I did. I whispered to her, "Hey, baby, Yvonne is working too hard. I need to do something special for her. I will make sure you are very happy later." Yvonne must have heard what I said. She started to fast-jerk and pressure-suck my cock. I went off like a rocket. I thought it was going to blow the back of her head off. But she just coughed a little then looked up at us and said, "Thank you." Julia smiled and reached over to steal some come from the head of my cock and licked it off her fingers. I said to Yvonne, "You are very welcome, baby. Now stand up, I want to show you how welcome you are." She stood up and I kissed her then I kissed Julia.

We all three kissed on each other trying to keep our lips together while sharing some leftover secretion saliva. Then I said to Yvonne, "Now, bend over baby, you have done so much for everybody else I think it's time I give you some doggie flavor. Julia smiled. Yvonne smiled and bent over. I laid her skirt up over her ass on her lower back. Oops, guess what, no panties. I said, "EEM, Easy entrance, reach for your toes baby." She did and I wasn't wasting any time. I knew it wouldn't be long until another load got dropped but that was okay. I shoved my cock as deep and as far in that split-open-hole between her legs as it would go. I started pounding her pussy with a rapid-fire performance reaming from the side.

Dropping loads and experiencing orgasmic-bliss is what it was all about. I was pulling her ass back hard with my hands making sure I could dive as deep as possible. It didn't last long, but I liked it, she liked it and I blasted her pussy parlor with an over-load of come. I pulled out slowly, gently massaging both the tittys a little on the way. She stood up and turned around. I said, "Thank you, baby, and you are so welcome to every part of us. We want this to be the happiest birthday you could ever have." I added, "It's not over yet." And as I gave her a kiss, Julia bent down and gave my cock a couple of main vein vacuum sucks and said, "It's my turn, Larry. I want to give you a birthday present too." They traded places and so it was. It was kind of a short session but certainly not uneventful. I attended to her twat doggie style with about 20 hard fast pelvic-pumps and butt-cheek slaps, and she was fucked.

We all stood up and started straightening our clothes and making preparations to leave. When I shut the door to my locker, I saw we had some unexpected company. It was a young lady that I used to sing with in church choir.

I don't know how she managed to get to her locker without me seeing her walking up. Her name was Betty Sue. Her locker was about five away from mine which put it close to the stairway. I must've shut my eyes for a second or two when she was coming up the stairs.

I wonder what she thought, she must have heard something. I had tried to get better acquainted with her while we were in the choir but was not successful.

She just looked at us and smiled. She said hello and ask if we were having fun. Yvonne knew her pretty well so she told her that we were all getting ready to go out and celebrate my birthday and ask if she would like to come along. She declined the invitation, smiled, and told us to have fun, then wished me a happy birthday as she was leaving.

We all looked at each other and made a couple of silent thank you "God" statements, then headed out to the parking lot. We decided to take Yvonne's car because it was larger. She was driving the family station wagon and there was room for all three of us in the front seat.

I, of course, chose to sit in the middle. I always liked to keep my mind free and both hands busy when possible. When I could sit between two Split-tails like these, I could accomplish my objectives very easily.

We had been cruising around for about 45 minutes. I had been having considerable success in pleasuring both pussy's. With a slight leg spread, they became eager and easily accessible to my middle fingers.

The tits and nipples were a little more difficult, especially Yvonne's, because she was driving. Sucking or orally massaging tits and nipples when your grazing ground is interfering with the automobile's path of travel could be a little frustrating and quite possibly even dangerous.

Julia, however, was a different story. She was totally accessible, even for fucking. She loved the word fucking almost as much as she loved to fuck. Sometimes while the three of us were involved in our activities, Julia would just start pronouncing that word. And say it in different ways and use it in different sentences. Sometimes she would just spell the word **f-u-c-k**. It almost seemed like she was obsessed with the word. Julia would also confess to us how many different objects she had used to penetrate her pussy or to fuck herself with.

She especially liked using vegetables such as carrots, cucumbers, beans, celery, and green onions. She had even tried potatoes, an ear of corn, and the smaller crooked neck squash. But she said they were a little more difficult to achieve pussy penetration with. Julia possessed a vegetable swallowing **split-tail/pussy.** If you were to ask her how her garden grows, she would take great pleasure in explaining every little detail. Right down to just how deep the bend of the crook-necked squash would permit penetration before she would get frustrated and forcefully jam it all the way inside to provide more pleasurable pain for her climax. Or how she'd get pissed off at the bean or green onion because they were too limber and sometimes they ended up in her ass-hole instead of her pussy. She, at her young age, could and quite possibly should have been considered a verbal artist for the pictures she would orally paint while bringing to reality the description of the way she abused her vegetable pussy partners.

Chapter 5
"Orgiastic Bliss"

I leaned over to Julia's ear and whispered, "I'll be right back." I gave her pussy four or five energetic finger pumps. Then reaming her pussy lips slowly, I removed my right hand. I turned my body a little bit toward Yvonne and provided her pussy a similar move with my left hand. I put Yvonne's pussy flavor saturated fingers in my mouth and licked off the juices. Then I took my right hand with Julia's pussy flavored fingers and placed them to Yvonne's lips, which she immediately performed a secretions-suck-off process.

Once Yvonne had secured Julia's love juices, I started to remove my fingers. I realized right away when she bit down on my fingers that she might be a little upset. I made sure she understood I was not going to neglect her.

Usually, there was no problem with the competitive spirit of these two split-tails, but I noticed a little difference today. Maybe it was because it was my birthday and they both wanted to make sure they gave me the same kind of present.

Adjusting my body position a little more toward Yvonne, I was able to massage both her tittys as well as providing adequate nipple-pinching pleasure. My total attention was now on Yvonne. I was trying to perform her pleasures satisfactorily without causing her a driving problem.

I was right-handed and that made it much easier for me to perform the perfect pussy puncture. I penetrated her first with the forefinger of my right hand. I Did a little exploring then popped my middle finger in. I double finger fucked her gently while applying a push massage with my thumb on the area just above her clitoris. I started a reaming roll procedure on her vaginal opening and she spread her legs a little farther. I then incorporated the third finger for more pressure pleasure and began a much faster and high-powered finger fuck.

With every pump, Yvonne's left knee would bang over against the door. She was really getting into it.

Suddenly, I got an idea of the experimental nature. I knew we had done a little butt-hole insinuating back in the days of our touchy-feely processes. I gradually slowed down the rapid-fire-finger-fuck to a crawl. Yvonne gave a little moan, and as I pulled out my fingers, she whimpered. I jammed my thumb all the way into her cunt. She sucked her stomach in and her mouth opened as though she was gasping for air. My fingers had plenty of lubrication and I went straight up the crevice between her ass cheeks and lubricated her butt-hole. I started ream-rolling the rim of her ass-hole. She sucked her stomach in farther and held her breath harder and her eyes got really big. I was working my thumb vigorously inside and around the walls of her pussy while tease-tapping her clit from time to time. I could feel Yvonne tightening the seal with her butt-hole muscle. She was protecting it as though it had never been breached before. I guess she forgot about the play-times of yesteryear.

It didn't take very long before she was starting to relax a little. I could tell the time was right. I began pilfering with the make-believe virgin status of Yvonne's anal opening by the playful popping of her prune. I continued my invigorating thumb to pussy pleasuring and brought my fingers back to the bottom part of her pussy to replenish the lubricating love juices. Then I returned to her ass-hole with my middle finger and very fast force-fed it two knuckles deep into her anal-opening. Yvonne kind of butt-jump-bounced two or three times and held her breath again. I forced my finger in over that knuckle a little deeper and bent it in toward my thumb. Yvonne grunted, "Oh my!" Her mouth was stuck on open as though she had lockjaw or was singing Christmas carols. She was gasping for air. I could feel my middle finger and thumb rubbing together on the thin sheath that separated her vaginal canal from her ass-hole. Together, we were working the in and out finger fucking process in her pussy and her butt-hole in perfect rhythm. My fingertips were nearly touch-rubbing, romancing each other through the very thin separating skin.

The look on Yvonne's face was one of disbelief with the background of happiness. Her eyes got big and her mouth opened wider and she suddenly started revolving her entire butt and pussy body parts back and forth then around. Realizing what was going on, Julia had started jacking me off. She was trying to get her mouth in the right position to suck my cock. I started Yvonne's rhythmized double penetration finger fuck procedure, going with a little more vigor. She began to bounce around releasing unusual mouthing sounds as well as pussy farts and ass-hole rumbles. Julie had succeeded in swallowing the head of my cock and providing it with a very satisfying rim tongue and lip massage blow-job.

I felt a bump, like the car just ran off the road. Thank "God" Yvonne had found a wide spot at the side of the road where she pulled off and stopped. She was bouncing up-down and around like crazy, screaming, oh my "God," oh my "God," oh my "God," while at the same time pulling very forcefully at the steering wheel and her hair with one hand as she tugged at my shirt with the other. I knew she was having an attack of orgasmic bliss. But I did not know which of her bodily orifices would be the first to receive the blessing. I just kept the double-penetration finger-fucking process going. I was hoping it would provide a more painfully pleasurable release of her well-deserved and overdue come-droppings.

I looked over at Julia; she was sucking my cock and finger fucking herself. I stretched up and gave Yvonne a lip-lock with high powered tongue-sucking action. She broke away scream-jumping and her butt was sliding toward the front of the car, pushing hard against my fingers. I could feel her butt muscles tighten around my middle finger. My thumb and the palm of my hand got saturated by a bountiful blessing of the warm wetness from her pussy's love-juice. My prick turned into a come fountain. I gave a couple of jerky grunts as Julia increased the suction and tightened her mouth around the rim of my cock. She was swallowing my come and exploded orgasmically all over her hand and the seat. Fortunately for all of us, the seat covers were plastic. What a perfect birthday present, the three of us laying in a triplet-love nest-liaison of orgiastic wonders.

Fortunately, Yvonne had picked a good place to pull the road. There was nobody around, just a big wide spot in the road. We all looked at each other and smiled, and they said together, "Happy birthday, Larry." I replied, "Thank you both very much!!! What a present. Wow, can we do that again?" They both responded at the same time with, "Why, hell yes, Larry. You know you can have us both anytime you want to as long as we all do it together. When did you have in mind?" I replied, "That is the only thing that makes this so much fun and so good. Just think, we started this stuff all together a long time ago. It was fun then and it's fun now. Maybe we should all three just get married. We could have a ball fucking and making love for the rest of our lives.

There's a restaurant just a few miles up the road. They have curb service or you can eat inside. Let's go there and get a coke so we can take a little time to think about what just happened and decide when we want to do it again." Everybody agreed so we went to the restaurant.

Chapter 6
"Hot Dog Horny"

I think we all had to go to the bathroom to wash whatever and perform the necessary bathroom functions. We had chosen to stay inside instead of ordering from the car, mainly because they had booths and we could all three sit in the same seat. I, of course, claimed rights to the middle seat. I had come to realize it was much more pleasurable for all concerned when I was stuck between two split-tails, especially these two.

One thing I loved about Yvonne and Julia was they always came ready to play. They were like that from our very first time several years ago. And they never followed the same rules for the same game. I think they like the excitement of mixing up the manner in which one reaches one's points of interest. They never left me out in the dark. They were always very quick to instruct me on where their switches were located and which way to flip a particular switch to gain maximum sexual pleasure and performance.

The three of us were just sitting around shooting the shit. Or as Julia so elegantly put it, "We were fucking enjoying the fuck out of the flavors fucking seeping from our thoughts about the events of the past fucking couple of hours. How much fucking fun can three people have in one fucking hour?"

Yvonne brought up Betty Sue and we all started laughing. That of course instigated an episode of butt- bumping and hand-surfing each other's bodies so fast the waitress couldn't tell what we were doing.

Yvonne said, "I wonder what Betty Sue thought was going on, or if she heard anything?" I jokingly came back with, "Well if she saw or heard anything maybe it will help her disposition, and the next time she'll accept our offer to join us. Hell, she might have busted loose and had a little fun while she was learning how to enjoy everyone's body parts." Julia's hand went straight to my crotch and grabbed a handful of cock and balls as she said, "You fucker, this was our fuckin' birthday present to you and you fuckin' want someone else to fucking join in? Fuck you, Larry. You wouldn't be happy if you were fucking involved in an orgy with all the fuckin' fucked-up girls in the fucking high school. I ought to pull your fucking pecker off your simple little mother-fucker. Yeah, I'll bet you'd probably like to fuck some of the mothers in that fucking high school and probably already fucking have. Fuck-fuck- fuck, that's all that's on your mind." And she squeezed my cock-an-balls harder then poked me in the ribs with her elbow. I leaned over and gave her a little kiss-peck on the cheek and replied, "Julia-baby, don't blame me. I was just making a comment. Yvonne is the one that invited her." Yvonne poked my other rib cage and pinched my nipple. I continued with, "I can't help it, girls. I love pussy. You two fine lookin' little split-tails turned me into a cunt-licker many shinning-moons ago and got me addicted to it."

Julia called the waitress over and ordered two plain hotdogs and asked her to please not burn them. I had an order of French fries. Yvonne said she didn't want anything; she was going to share Julia's hotdogs.

We kept talking about the events of the afternoon and several things that were going to happen between now and graduation. I asked them if they heard where they were going to be working or if they had a job. Yvonne informed me they had both passed the test and was accepted by the FBI. They would be working In DC. I told them that's where I was headed and I hoped we could have our border-line out of the ordinary illicit kinky little sex get-togethers every now and then.

Julia's hand was still in my crotch and she put a gentle little squeeze on my nuts. I think she had glue on her hand when she put it there because she wasn't about to move it. I was okay with that; it kind of served as a comforting gesture after what she had said to me just a few minutes earlier.

The waitress brought our order and I reached over and got the ketchup bottle and doused my French fries. Then I handed the bottle over to Julia. She said, "No thanks, I eat it plain and without bread; it's too fattening with extras."

Then she passed one of the hotdogs over to Yvonne. They both at the same time made sure the hotdog was not hot enough to burn their fingers. Then they took the hotdog out of the bun, lifted it toward their lips, and blew it a little to cool it down.

That in itself could create a talking point for later if you perceive the shape of the hotdog and the pucker on their lips as a teasingly torturing taunt of forth-coming possible pleasures for sensual sex.

I looked at Julia, then I looked at Yvonne. They both winked. I couldn't really tell if they were winking at me or at each other. Yvonne kind of mimicked me a kiss as she was pretending to perform a lip massage to the end of the naked hotdog. She held it just far enough away from her mouth to keep from burning her lips in case it was still too hot. Julia was a little braver; she began a titillating tongue-tap to the bare beginning of the hotdog while squeeze-rolling my cock a couple times in the process.

They carefully kiss caressed their hotdog-peckers for a few seconds or more to make sure they had cooled down enough not to burn them. Then at the same time, both Julia and Yvonne started sensually giving the hotdog a blow-job. They used a very sexy looking turn-on-ish slow-blow and pucker-lip-suck so I could enjoy the hot-dog-dick cooling process as well.

They had very obviously done this before. In my mind, I felt if that was true they were more likely to have been screwing each other with the hot-dogs before eating them. It was kind of a turn-on to imagine they were screwing themselves in the mouth with each other's pussy-juice saturated hotdog munchy-mouth dill-doe.

I had eaten about half of my French fries and they were still doing the rolling-cooling in and out sucking the heat off their hotdogs. I looked over at Yvonne and said, "Sweetheart, if you're looking for something to suck I have something that you could have a lot more fun with and I would enjoy it more as well." Julia once again gave me bump in the rib cage with her elbow and squeezed my nuts as she told me, "We are fucking getting them ready to fucking feed to you Larry. We would fuckin' like them to be cool enough they don't fucking damage the tender touch of your fucking cunt-licking tongue and lips. After all, Larry baby, those are our fucking pussy pleasuring lips. We fuckin' would not want to cause them any fucking unnecessary pain." They both smiled and said, "This is the next phase of your birthday present honey. Our little life-long cunt-licking friend, you might call it the protein phase." I was kind of surprised, they were speaking in sync and Julia never said the word fuck once. Then Yvonne looked over at Julia and asked, "Honey, how much protein does pussy juice have in it?" Julia replied, "I'm not fucking sure, I'm just hoping that it fucking supplies him with enough fuckin' energy that he can make it through the rest of his fucking birthday surprises."

That's when I realized what they were getting ready to do. They had no panties on. I think this had all been planned, but when would they have planned it? They both had this "we got something for you, Larry" look on their face along with a sneaky little grin. They were going to fuck themselves with plain hotdogs and feed them to me. That would probably be the most uniquely strange yet ravishingly romantic birthday present I would ever get in my entire life.

I love doubling my pleasure and they liked doubling it for me. I couldn't help myself. I looked over at Julia and said, "Didn't you just tell me that I was fuck-crazy? Excuse me, but aren't you getting ready to fuck yourself with a fuckin' hotdog? Why didn't you go for a carrot, a stick of celery, hell even a cucumber would be an exciting way to explore the taste of a new salad dressing." She replied with her hand by squeezing my cock hard and painfully grind-rolling my nuts at the same time. Then she said, "We're fucking doing this for your sake, Larry. You get more fucking energy from eating meat than fuckin' vegetables and you fucking know we all three like to fuckin' waste lots of energy eating each other's fucking meat. Birthday-boy, you are fucking going to need all the energy you can fuckin' come up with before your fucking special day is fuckin' over. So shut the fuck up and give your fuckin' mouth a rest. You are going to fuckin' need it later too."

Fortunately, without going into detail, I will allow your imagination to run wild because that is just what we did. I will tell you we all lived through it and were able to attend our graduation ceremony. Oh, by the way, we got kicked out of the drive-in restaurant and the manager ask us never to return. I guess he felt sorry for his hotdogs. Maybe he was afraid they were going to drown and would have to live in **Split-Tail-Heaven** forever, being totally submerged in love lava. **The lucky fuckin' dogs. ***(???)**

After I graduated from high school, I got a job at the local Chevrolet garage and started working on my future connections with some of the new rising juniors and seniors. After about a year and a half, I moved to Maryland and got a job. I directed all my leftover energy to pursue my second job **(Split-tails),** which seemed to require more time to be spent in earnest than my real job, especially knowing my mental mandate could not, or would not, be denied. So, to avoid resorting to self-satisfaction through the means of masturbation, I set my sights, took aim, and shot my waad!!!

Chapter 7
"Lust At First Sight"

The news and novelty store I was working at was open until 11 PM. I had trained for the late shift because nobody else wanted it. I knew it would work out perfectly for me as far as the time requirement. The late shift also presented me with the opportunity to meet damn near everybody in town.

The store carried in stalk everything from candy bars to condoms. The owner made sure his inventory would include everything other stores in town carried and more.

The first **split-tail** that really got my attention after I started working there was almost at the closing time of my fourth day. The past three nights after I got off from work, I had depended on one of my former classmates for a hand job, blow job, and a fast fuck in the backseat of my car to satisfy my mind and body.

In case you're wondering how I just happened to run onto a former classmate, I guess a lot of people from my hometown came to this area for work and entertainment. There sure as hell was nothing exciting or otherwise happening back there.

After seeing this young lady, I was determined to add her to my list for possible pleasures, then she could be a recipient of my daily discharge demands.

She was a very beautiful young lady. She had long black shiny hair that lay in perfect waves of invitation and seemed to say as it traveled to the small of her back and came to rest comfortably on her buttocks. "Hey Larry, check out my hard-on-maker **ass**!". She had a perfect cock-sucker mouth with that protrusion point on her upper lip that massages your main vein when you are tangled up in a 69'er. Another of her prize 69'er possessions was an esophagus that loudly pronounced her desire for energetic "E" Train travel. She had tits that talked, high cheekbones, and eyes that walked through your mind, tearing it up and leaving memoir memories behind.

I was suddenly overcome with a deep driving desire to partake of the forbidden fruits she so magnificently displayed. I wanted some of that! I could just picture her sitting on my face and making herself heavy while I was tongue-slapping her Red-**Snapper.**

I noticed she had been wandering around the store as though she was just wasting time looking at different items. I decided to try to instigate a conversation. She must have heard me coming because as I approached, she turned around and smiled.

I said, "Good evening, young lady, my name is Larry and I'm a clerk here. Are you looking for something in particular? Maybe I could help you find what you're looking for." She replied, in a very low almost inaudible whisper, "Why, thank you, Larry, but I believe I just found what I was looking for." I noticed she had nothing in her hands and wasn't looking at anything so I inquired. "Oh, yeah, that's good, what is it?" She came back with those invitational eyes of sin and desire in a low seductively sultry voice and kinda whispered, "Why, Larry, I'm surprised, you didn't realize, I've been looking for you."

It sort of took me by surprise but I tried not to let it show. I responded with, "Well, I sure am glad I found you because it seems like we've been looking for each other without knowing it."

Her voice got sexier and her eyes projected an overflowing lustful desire of sin and sex as she said, "I knew I had to have you when I saw you walk through these doors this afternoon when you came to work. That's why I waited until later to come in.

I was hoping we would have fewer interruptions to cause problems with our introductions. Oh, by the way, my name is Kristi with a K and an I, and I am very pleased to meet you."

I was a little uncertain of what was going on but quite aware of the burning sensations taking place in sensitive areas of my body, specifically my groin. So I said, "My shift ends in about 20 minutes. Look around and waste some time. Maybe we can go somewhere and have a drink or talk a little, if that's okay with you." She said, "Yeah, that's fine, sounds really nice. I'll be right outside in my car just waiting for you." I didn't know what the hell to think but I couldn't wait to find out what we were doing for each other.

The next few minutes seemed to never pass. Kristi with a K and an I was acting like she knew me. Maybe we both have that same look of sex on our face and sin in our eyes and she noticed it in me as I had noticed it in her. I know one thing, I would find out very soon whether it was bull-shit or bona-fide.

11 o'clock finally made it. As I locked the door and turned around, there she stood. She was leaning back against the side of her car with her hands resting on the fenders at both sides of her money-maker. I walked up to her and said, "Damn, Kristi with the K and an I, I sure hope you don't mind me saying this right now but I just can't help myself. You look fucking good enough to eat." She smiled, then with a questioning look in her sin-filled eyes, she asked, "You promise?"

That's all it took, I very energetically said, "Baby, I don't think we need anything to drink. And I never make a suggestion jokingly not to do something I love to do. Especially with a gorgeous piece of female flesh like you. I fully intend to follow that dream and enjoy the pleasures of your pulsating pussy as it massages my tongue. Let's get the fuck outta here." She responded with, "This is my car, you drive." I said, "I'd rather not." She replied, "I think you'd better, I'm in the mood for a sample."

We no sooner got seated and I was ready to pull away from the curb as she reached over and grabbed my hand and I stopped. She leaned over and gave me little kiss-peck on the side of the cheek and said, "You are sexier now than you were the first time I saw you. My "God" you're exuding it. It's like seeping through your skin."

I reached over and pulled her to me. Her mouth became an overcharged magnet and I slapped a lip lock on her that included a special session of tongue tapping and tease-biting, then I responded with, "It's your fault, Kristi with a K and an I. I have been drooling from one orifice or another since the first time you caught my eye in the shop. You better loosen your lust until we can get somewhere to take care of business."

Take care of business is exactly what we did. But there was no way she was going to loosen her lust. If anything, it got tighter, much like her hand as she squeezingly seized my prick. I had no sooner pulled away from the curb and started to turn the corner at the end of the street when she unzipped my pants and grabbed my cock with both hands. The next thing I know, I could feel her head bumping up against the bottom of the steering wheel as she played her part in our business by draining my drool.

About three blocks away, there was a print shop that had been out of business for quite some time. Behind it was an alley and a small parking lot with very little lighting. I figured that would be the perfect place to insert my interest in this partnership.

The car she was driving was a rambler ambassador and the seats laid all the way down. Maybe that's why she bought it. It sure as hell didn't make any difference to me; I was glad we had it. Because the next hour and a half we were like two wild animals exercising absolutely no control over their partaking of and devouring all possible body parts pertaining to the pleasures of pussy and prick.

I had absolutely no explanation for what was going on and didn't want one. It was happening, and as far as I was concerned, our business was pleasuring each other and our business was being taken care of.

It was like fire on fire, wet on water, or hot on hot. By pulling, ripping, biting, and scratching, we stripped each other's body of all that was hiding them, including my socks. We wanted to see naked, we wanted to touch naked.

We had slipped feverishly into the number (69) position and Kristi was power sucking the head of my cock while blowing my mind by painfully pleasuring my balls with both hands. She would squeeze-role and shift hands while tease-biting the head of my cock and nibble-nipping the cock-rim and main vein. I had buried my nose as deep as it would go into her ass-hole. By shape-stretching my tongue to be pointed, I could barely reach the bottom part of her split-spread wide open pussy lips.

I had been performing a tit massage by pinch-rolling her nipples with both hands. Suddenly, my animal anger surfaced and my interests changed with the full submergence of one of Kristi's fingers into my ass-hole. I had no idea or no warning it was going to happen. That was the first time it happened unexpectedly since Jean. But she had been so much more gentle with me in every way.

I was still top-side with my nose in her ass and my tongue gently teasing her twat. But all of a sudden, I wanted to inflict pain on her. I mean powerful pissed-off punishment pain. It was almost like one move, I twisted my body with reckless abandon for pain from her finger exiting my ass-hole, or her teeth slide-biting my cock, or her hands squeezing my nut-sack with powerful individual-ball appreciation.

About the time her chin slid off the front seat toward the floor, I gave her ass a hard slap and spit on her prune. I spread her ass-cheeks, and with the full force of my motor thrust, my prick deep into her anal cavity, and they became one. She screamed very loud as her head came up and hit the bottom of the dash. I didn't give a shit, I just wanted to hurt her. For about the next five minutes,

I was flat-out force-fucking her in the ass-hole with my rock-hard cock. I mean I was power-pounding that prune.

She should not have stuck her finger up my ass like that. I leaned forward a little bit, raising my ass up, then gave my cock a little twist in her butt-hole and she screamed again. I leaned back a little to keep my head from banging the roof of the car and brought my left leg around and pressed down hard on her upper back. I press-rolled her tit's flat on the seat until she gave a loss of breath grunt-scream. Now I had good leverage so I leaned back a little more to keep my head from hitting the roof. Then with my right hand I, consciously angry, slammed three fingers as far inside her cunt as they would go.

For the next minute or two, I was engaged in a dual fucking process. Pussy or prune, which one should I pound with the most power? Trying not to play favorites, I began the best prune pounding and forceful finger fucking contest I could administer. At which time she began to cry, then she screamed, "Oh, baby-fuck me-fuck me, you are so good to me, fuck me deep."

This wasn't working, she was enjoying it. I started coming back to my senses and began to ease up a bit and started to exit her ass-hole slowly. As I got almost all the way out, she beggingly cried, "Oh no, please stay, fuck me, please fuck me in the ass, go deep, deep, deeper." Finally, I asked her, "Doesn't it hurt?" She cried out, **"Yes, yes it hurts, but it feels so good when it hurts. Do-it, do-it, do it, do it deeper-deeper-deeper.** I just kept cock-an-ball slapping her ass-crack. I filled her anal cavity with an eight-inch rock-hard and growing cock. I answered every moaning request she made for more with a proud prick ream-lubing wall process of creamy cramming.

I knew soon I would be fudge-packing so I filled her ass with orgasmic gas and she finally farted. Her body was shaking so hard I thought she was having an orgasm. Then I finally realized she was crying and laughing at the same time so I gently removed our connection then turned her over and said, "Are you alright?"

Almost breathless, she replied, "I'm fine, you are so good to me, and so good for me. Now it is my turn, I must return your love favors. What is your preference? Lay down, Larry, relax, and let me love you."

With that she took my entire cock-shaft in her mouth and began to lick and suck it clean of all extra juices or what-ever excrement might have been present. She lifted her head a little, allowing my cock to slip out from between her soft juicy lips and said, "You are exactly what I wanted you to be. You are exactly what I needed you to be. Somehow, I knew you would be, I don't know how, but I did."

I pulled her close to me and held her gently for a few seconds. Her head was bowed. I put my fingers under her chin and lifted her face even with mine. Her beautiful brown eyes showed signs of tearing. Ever so apologetically I tenderly kissed her soft, juicy lips.

We held each other for a short time. Remaining quiet, while enjoying the scenery of our nudity by the little to no light provided. It was almost like lying on the beach naked under a dark moon.

She started to make her move on my cock and balls in repayment for what she called my great performance. I stopped her and said, "Let's just lay back and enjoy the scenery and talk a little bit. You can pay me back later. In fact, you don't owe me anything, I owe you an apology."

The first thing I asked her was, "Have you always liked painful sex? I am normally not a hurtful person but you made me do it." She replied, "That's the way it all got started for me. I have really never liked it any other way. Quite honestly, I have not really known anything else. You were fantastic, I loved it. Now it's my turn, as I told you." I said, "No-no it's okay, just relax if you can. I will fondle your features mentally and physically while I tell you a story."

I began with, "I love to fuck, I love to eat pussy. I was once referred to as the best little cunt-licker in town. I like sex anyway it can happen, but I do not like violent sex. If you had not jammed your finger into my ass-hole without warning or lubrication, none of this would've happened." She responded with, "Yeah and I would have never got the fuck of my life. Man, you fucked the dog shit outta me. Larry, you are that good-looking piece-a-cock I have been shopping for and I can't wait for it to happen again. I had an orgasm from every opening in my body. I think I even came through my ears. Every pressure point was triple heart-beat throbbing. I thought my whole body was going to explode. You made that happen for me. Baby, you are not only handsome, but you are also absolutely wonderfully beautiful. And besides that, you got a really nice cock."

Then I asked her, "So you're a cock shopper? How long have you been shopping for me?" She replied, "Ever since the first time I saw you."

I asked, "And when was that?" She said, "At your homecoming dance. You were the Queen's escort, which means you were probably voted homecoming King, that is usually the way it goes. I am pretty sure they don't pick their own escorts or at least they didn't at our school. I'm surprised you didn't notice me. I couldn't take my eyes off you." I came back with, "My 'God', that was a year and a half ago. You could've said something before now." She jumped in with, "Yes, I suppose I could have just walked up to you and said, hey baby, you want to have a good time. Or maybe be a little more subtle and say, let's fuck." I replied, "You could have done either, but you chose not to. Why?" She responded with, "I guess I just needed to gather a little more information.

I had a couple of friends that knew you. They were at the dance and they noticed that I was taking quite an interest in you." I said, "Who were they?" She said, "Oh, you wouldn't know them. They're my age." I asked, "Did they have any information for you?" She replied, "Yeah, quite a bit." I said, "Well, Kristi with a K and an I, why in the hell don't you just tell me everything they said, then I will know who they are. If I didn't know them they wouldn't have anything to tell you, right?"

She told me who they were. And I immediately responded with, "You're right, I don't know them. So how the hell could they tell you anything about me?" Which was a lie, I knew them both. They were both former playmates. One of them was Jean and I didn't think I should go there. She said, "I think they knew someone you used to see or something like that."

Kristi didn't seem to want to discuss it anymore. She had twisted her body partially to one side and began a crazy duet of toe and cock sucking. Then she positioned herself in an unconnected 69 and would float from toe to cock. Lip and tongue suck-sliding all the way up one leg to a cock and ball kiss caressing maneuver and back down the other one to my feet and toes.

I was doing just what she asked me to, laying back and enjoying it all. Then suddenly, I felt one hand slide up the crack of my ass and come to rest as one lonesome finger seemed to have gotten lost and began rim-tapping my ass-hole in search of a place it could just pop-in and hang out, (or) have a party. I immediately reached down, took her hand, and rubbed it all around on the inter-lips of her pussy. Then I took her hand and put it in my mouth, extracting all excess juices and returned it back to her pussy. Using her hand and fingers, I told her that I encouraged female masturbation and I also loved to watch their response to being forced to finger-fuck themselves.

Once her pussy had secreted enough juices, I replaced her finger on my ass-hole and whispered quietly, "Let's try some lubrication this time, shall we?" She had no verbal response. She simply started a prepare and replace process from my ass-hole to her pussy to my mouth to her pussy to my ass-hole then penetrated.

Kristi was very quick at understanding what needed to be done. After a few minutes of her body washing, cock sucking, ball blazing, and gentle prune puncturing, she had positioned herself perfectly so I could spread her pussy lips open

wide enough to swallow my mouth. Using my fingers, I parted her pussy lips so that my entire mouth was surrounded by them. This allowed me to render her somewhat unconscious with a clit-lip caress and inner pussy-wall tongue swirl.

After a minute or two of working this whirlwind clit-clamp procedure, Kristi's entire body started a quivering quake process that scrambled her muscle control. She had a blowout orgasm that filled my mouth and almost forced me to swallow my tongue as she vigorously tried to cover my entire face with her pussy. I somehow managed to keep my lips in pussy eating position, enough to try restoring possession of her clit and inner pussy wall. That just was not going to happen. Kristi was too busy bouncing around breast bruising and nipple pinching. On occasion, she would slap herself or pull at her hair. She would take her fingers and scratch her stomach so hard red tracking fingernail trails appeared across her tightening tiny little tummy.

She was going insane, bouncing up and down so hard she almost knocked my teeth out when they made contact with her pussy. It was so obvious she wanted to feel pain or abuse of some nature. So I took the thumb from my right hand and stuck it in between her lips. As she secured it to sucking status, she bit it so hard I yelled, "You mother- fucking--cock-sucking little cunt. You want to feel pain, try this on for size." I yanked my thumb from between her teeth and with one power-push drove it deeply into her ass-hole. It went so far up her anal cavity my wrist would not permit deeper penetration.

Kristi let out a deafening scream and immediately juice-i-fied my nostrils. She just kept screaming, bouncing, and flooding my nose. I had reverted back to my hurtful demeanor and was slap pounding her ass-hole. Kristi had a constant orgasmic flow and just kept coming and coming and coming.

I found it very hard to say I was not enjoying her pain. She just kept begging for more. She would say, "Go deeper and deeper, give me more." I, being pissed off and always eager to painfully please, ripped my thumb from her ass-hole with jet-propelled speed. That created a vacuum-popping sound followed by a fart before I could jam my fore-finger and middle finger deep into her anal opening to plug its passage.

I jam-packed and repeatedly pushed my anal attentive double-digits deeper and deeper into Kristi's butt-hole. One might say I was doing my due-diligence for pain provision. She became overwhelmed and weakened from the pleasurable pain of her anal orifice and the exhausting process of many, mini-orgasms. Her kum-filled storage compartment had satisfyingly yet savagely surrendered the orgasmic-bliss of so much pain and ecstasy. I had succeeded in providing her with more than enough pleasure to drain all her bodily fluids and Kristi lay limp beside me on the seat.

I could feel my cock and my mind began to possess a little ego-swell. That didn't last long, and it was a little scary. I didn't know whether I hurt her so bad it caused this to happen or she had just passed out. I disengaged all our body parts and moved her towards me enough that I could open her eyes, and I asked her, "Are you okay?" No response so I repeated, "Kristi, Kristi, are you okay? Say something, baby, or I'm gonna take you to the hospital." She could barely open her eyes.

She looked up at me, then almost breathless and dove-eyed she said, "You are just too good to me, give me a moment and I'll be alright."

That sounded okay to me so I just kind of laid back the best I could in the bed like seats and rested a little. I guess it had been maybe five minutes when I noticed Kristi was starting to move around.

She was sitting on my lower abdomen and upper groin area with her back to me. Her head was almost resting on the dashboard. She was attempting to rejuvenate my cock to hard-on status with her hands. I said, "Stick it in your mouth or cram it in your cunt, it'll be hard in a heartbeat. You know, suck it or fuck it, hell I can play with it." As she teasingly tracked her pussy up toward my face I could feel a trail of her twat Juices mapping out my body.

She knew exactly what she was doing. She brought her body to a halt with her pussy and ass-hole positioned perfectly for my potential viewing and chewing pleasures. Kristi's pussy lips were wide open, lying loose and lusciously aroused to dampness. Her pussy was releasing little drops of smoldering-hot-sex-lava onto my chest between my tits. Kristi left me laden with nothing but lust for a taste-test of her tantalizingly tormenting twat of temptation.

How might I this woman's wonders measure, if only I could crawl inside, for her I know I would provide, permanent and perfectly polished pleasure.

Kristi then started a lip massage sucking process of playing with my foreskin and nibble-nipping the head and rim of my cock. It felt really nice and soothing. I tried to delay the hardness so I could enjoy it a little longer. At a certain point, there was nothing I could do, my cock got hard.

Cocks tend to do that when they are being attended to by a really good cock-sucker or lovemaking partner that knows what they are doing. And Kristi, with a K and an I, definitely knew what the hell she was doing. She also knew what the viewing position of her pussy and ass-hole was doing to my mental. **It was being mentally measured for framing and permanent placement among my memeried-memoirs in my wonderful world of afterglow. And still, to this day, holds perfection status** *for my eyes only!!!*

I tried to play a little game with her. Since we were in kind of a 69'er, I went for her pussy first. I also knew what she really wanted. I took my right hand and wiped up the leftover love-lava from my body then inserted the same two fingers into her pussy for added juices.

There was no doubt in my mind what was going to happen when I made physical contact with her ass-hole. Whether it be my nose, my tongue, my fingers, or my cock. It had become quite obvious to me that Kristi was a Prune lady, with a capital P. The body part or object used to penetrate the prune made very little difference to her.

I really didn't think she could have any type of sex and enjoy it without having something stuck up her ass that was just kind of hanging out there. It must have restored memories of satisfaction from the start of that very special and precious addiction. Kristi had obviously received a lot of back-door-slamming with pleasurable pain during her sexual encounters of yore.

She must have been the recipient of many dominant, or maybe even demanding, influential anal entries, to have developed the treasured prune fetish that she has. I guess it could've been somebody it shouldn't have been, maybe somebody older or somebody she looked up to. I tried to get her to tell me how it all started. I had made up my mind this time I would try to bring her pleasure and hope while doing so I could forget about her pain.

I had just started massaging her pussy lips and tickling her clit with my tongue when she began to move her butt up and down. She would go down until her pussy was almost on my chest. My nose made contact with her ass-hole. My chin was massage-pleasuring the lips on her ***smokin'-hot -snatch-of-suduction*** on each up-and-down stroke.

I knew it was time so I took my fingers and started massaging her anal gland. It only took a couple of strokes and she insisted on entrance.

Kristi started applying ass-hole tightening pressure to the end of my fingers and flexing her butt muscles.

Chapter 8
"Switch Hitting"

After about a minute of her unusual chin-massaging anal-squeezing process, she became a switch hitter. She took both box's, her pussy and her prune, in search of my cock and fucked herself silly.

It was equally important for her to achieve orgasmic bliss from both pleasure-seeking places. Sometimes it seemed to me that she got more pleasure and satisfaction from pain induced by anal sex. I kind of thought that to be a little strange, but maybe her sex organs got reversed at birth, who knows. All I know and all I care about is Kristi, with a K and an I, can damn sure work it.

Kristi's upper torso was mostly being supported by the dashboard now and her head was resting on the dash. Her back was fully to my view. My feet were on the floor and my legs remained rather tightly fit together. She had arranged it so my nut-sack would be as accessible as my cock.

Then she started to make a massaging maneuver on my cock and balls with her hands. When she sat straight up on my lap to perform that maneuver, she had to tilt her head a little to keep it from hitting the roof of the car. Kristi had been very proficient in providing the pleasures to secure my pricks full staff status. Her feet and legs were on the outside of mine so that she could make sure my lap would be permanent enough to support her pleasures.

She was sitting mostly on my groin area and had made sure she had sufficiently lubricated both her pussy and her ass-hole. Then came the **switch-hitting!!!** Raising her butt a little, she was able to roll slightly to one side and achieve successful insertion in both her pussy and ass-hole without moving my body hardly at all. My cock was now serving as her pleasure pole for both holes.

This process of the same pole for both holes continued without full insertion for several minutes. I was now truly doing exactly what she wanted me to do, nothing. According to Kristi, I was going to be the recipient of physical payment for all the pleasurable pain I had bestowed upon her earlier.

All I was required to do was **stay-hard and keep-coming**. I had absolutely no problem with that. The youthful structure of my prick seemed to be about 90% in that of the erection state, and **coming-comes-easy** to a cock that is always being fucked, sucked, or played with.

Suddenly, I noticed that she had become considerably overzealous in her switch-hitting procedures. The proper positioning of my cock while switching from pussy to ass-hole had become more aggressive and very precise. My prick had been presented with the painful pleasures of double-joint lubrication by the demands of **constant-kum-droppings**. Kristi was body talking to me. With every twist, insertion, exit, reposition, rolling reinsertion, and butt-bounce, she was telling me what she wanted and how she was going to make it happen. She had made sure that my position would be perfect for providing the power and leverage for pain-filled pleasure to either love-hole she picked to penetrate. So I thought to myself, *I'll build a fire in her ass she'll never forget.*

She had just inserted my prick a little deeper into her pussy and leaned forward. I knew where the pressure would be coming from as I reached my hands around her body and very aggressively started a squeeze-grab-massage on her tits. I knew that she knew which way to lean and which hole should be favored in order to acquire the maximum presence of pleasurable pain because that's what she loved.

As I began my nipple-nip-pinch-n-roll and fast, hard tit-massaging process, I pulled her back towards my chest. I immediately started talking a little trash while tease-biting her ear, then slightly raised her ass a little. I could feel my main vein applying light pressure on her pussy lips as I moved her body up and jammed my rock-hard-cock deep into her cunt. Kristi's cunt channel started swelling with pride as my prick caused a continuous spreading to the walls of her pussy parlor. She began to rotate her ass vigorously. With her body jerking side to side, I could feel the main vein of my prick crushing her clit with every left to right rotation of her butt. I quickly dropped my right hand to the outside of her pussy so that I could pull back and apply more pressure on her clit. She gave a satisfying sigh of approval. I then stuck my middle finger partly inside of her pussy to apply more pressure on her clitoris as it slid across the main vein of my cock.

Kristi made a few more happy sounds and squeeze-rolled my nuts gently a few times in appreciation. I was bound and determined to somehow give her pussy a good fucking and hopefully administer a little pleasurable pain while doing so.

Hoping I could catch her a little off guard, I lifted my ass up and slid down so that with some leg Leverage, I could apply an upward curl to my ass and slam a home run hit on her clit. And so it happened. Kristi was bouncing around from side to side. Her head hit the roof of the car a couple of times. She immediately lubricated a finger and touched it faster than fast to my ass-hole and said, "I guess you know where I'm going." I immediately yanked my ass back and pulled my prick out of her pussy then set my sights on her ass-hole, then whispered softly, "Not if I get there first, baby." With full motor force, I slammed my entire cock-shaft almost balls and all as far up inside her ass-hole as it would go. Kristi screamed and her backbone curl forward as her head hit the roof of the car so hard I thought she broke her neck. She kept screaming and crying and bouncing up and down and back and forth then screamed at me, **"Oh, you dirty son-of-a-bitch**, I knew you had it in ya, I knew you could do it, you love-making butt-fuckin' bastard. Pump that prick, pound my prune with everything you got. Fuck me hard, hurt me, fucking hurt me bad, hurt me till it feels good." Then all of a sudden, with her head laying sideways on the roof, she lifted herself up enough to do a half twirl-split. Her left foot was lying over my shoulder and I could feel my cock reaming her ass-hole out while she was twirling. She went all the way around twice and back once. I guess she had to unwind her anal cavity.

Kristi just kept screaming and bouncing to a semi-twist twirl while screaming out, "Thank you, thank you, thank you!" Bouncing and twisting twirl's, saying again, "Thank you, I love it when you fuck me in the ass. Thank you, I fucking love you, thank you!" I really didn't want to hear that but I took it all in stride and laid back and did what she asked me to do.

Very relaxed, I started enhancing my love muscle by over-working my motor. I just laid there and pecker- pumped her prune. After a few minutes, I assisted her in turning her back to me again. Knowing this would be a hurtful position, with my cock still in her ass-hole, I reached up and **viciously squeeze-grabbed her tits** then pulled her back hard and fast flat against my chest. My cock was hard as a rock pushing her anal cavity almost through her stomach and out her bellybutton. I kept on pumping pecker and she kept on screaming, **"Do it, fucking do it--do it--do it, do it harder, do it deeper, do it now, just fucking like that, just like that, oh baby I like it up my ass, fuck my ass, do it baby, oooh-yeees, deeper-deeper-deeper drive it, drive it-drive, drive it home n-o-o-o-w baby."** I wrapped up all my strength and energy together and smacked her on the ass very hard twice with both hands. Then I gave her about 10 pile-driving, repeated pecker poundings. I must have busted my nuts 20 times as I committed

first-degree assault on the inside of her **ass-hole(or)anal-cavity(or) poop-shoot. Which-ever you prefer.**
??????????????????????????????

I knew it was time to rest. As I slowly slid my throbbing timber-member out of her ass-hole, she was not moving. I could feel my heart beating faster. My cock was stuck at hard-on status in a continual saluting mode. I began to have visions of grandeur of having an eternal hard-on.

I had succeeded in generating my multiple nut-busting and Kristi's orgasmic-explosions from Rear-Entry. In my mind that afforded me bragging rights for the most bodacious-blast of butt-fucking ever!!!

I turned her over on her back kissed her on the forehead and said, "I hope I've made you happy and I know you got your rocks. You know where you can find me, anytime you feel the need to go cock-shopping." Then I kissed her gently on the lips. She opened her eyes then smiled and exclaimed, "You're not going anywhere!" She quickly grabbed my cock along with one nut to secure my presence, then continued, "Larry baby is going home with Kristi. And Kristi is going to lock his butt- fucking cock up and tie him down. In other words, I am kidnapping your cock. So if you need to call anybody to let them know not to worry about you, perhaps you should do that when you see the next pay-phone."

I kissed her again and teasingly gave her teeth and gums some tender tongue travel. I continued my tongue trailing all around her tits and over her tummy. Up and down her thighs and very sensitive tight-tender-twat and said, "Now for dessert, lie still dear Kristi with a K an I and let **me**-- love **you**."

I continued to eat my fill which took a while. I guess I was just a born pussy eater and hers' was so appealing - nice, warm, wet, and very tasty. So tasty I couldn't resist taking her up on her offer to let her take me home and tie me up. I had never tried that before but I was sure with her it would have to be fun.

After my tongue recovered from pussy paralysis, we got dressed and she drove me back to pick up my car and I followed her home. She lived in Aspen Hill, just a short distance from where I lived in Suitland.

We hadn't taken much time for introductions or small talk so I suggested we stop and get a bite to eat. My suggestion was made by pulling into the parking lot of an all-night restaurant to see if she would follow me. She quickly turned around and came back. That told me she was serious about spending a little more time with me.

After we had been seated and placed our order, I stood up and excused myself so I could go to the restroom to wash my face and hands. When I returned, Kristi did the same. As she was returning to the table, our food arrived. We ate and drove to her place in her car.

On our way, she informed me that she had a roommate but she had her own bedroom and ask if I was okay with that. I said, "Sure, it's fine, I like girls, I mean young ladies, the more the merrier." She said, "It's late and she'll probably be in bed but you can meet her later. We will have to keep the noise down a little." I replied, "That's fine. I'll just stick something good in your mouth every time you start to scream." She smiled a little and said, "Uh-oh another promise."

When we got inside, she said, "Have a seat. I'll turn some music on and be right back. The bathroom is right at the end of the hall. Should you need to go make sure the door on your extreme left is closed once you're inside." I guess they shared a bathroom and it had doors opening into both bedrooms. I thanked her and told her I was fine and sat down on the couch to wait for her return.

While I was waiting, I looked around a little. From what I could see, it looked like a very nice and relatively new apartment or condo. I found out later it was categorized as a two-story condo.

She and her roommate had purchased it together and had it custom built. It had a California style pass-through kitchen bar, a very nice fireplace with a mantle and hearth. Between the kitchen and fireplace was a regular type bar with four stools.

When Kristi returned, she was wearing a robe. I said, "Wow, Kristi with a K and I, you're looking fine, and you think of everything. Not only do you make that robe look great but you made sure it was easily eliminated. Be careful, I might get used to this." She smiled and said politely, "Thank you, and I hope you take advantage of my eagerness to please efforts. I checked on my roommate while I was gone. She was watching TV and said she might come out a little later."

I nodded, my approval told her she had a nice place, and ask if the bar was open. She informed me, yes, that she was just getting ready to ask me if I wanted a drink. We both found our way to the bar. Kristi sat on a stool and I just leaned up against the bar so we could be a little closer as I touch-tested the softness of her partially open robe while we were talking.

I knew I had to find a way to tell Kristi who I thought the friend she was visiting in my hometown was, so I said, "You know, I think I do know the young lady you were visiting when you saw me at the homecoming dance.

You said her name was Jean Bonner. It must be the same person, and if it is, she used to be my babysitter when I was around nine years old. Rather, I guess you might say she kind of watched after me while my mother was working.

If it was her and she is still a friend, I would like to say hello sometime. I liked Jean, I'll never forget her. We had a lot of fun during those three or four years. Oh, by the way, Jean was four years older than I. If you are both the same age, that means I am four years younger than both of you. But that's fine, I love older women, most of the time they are very good teachers. And the more you know, the more I learn. I am always willing to learn more."

Kristi had gone over to the refrigerator to get some ice for the bar. As she was walking back, she responded by saying, "Sure, she is still my friend and I'm positive we can get together sometime. I know she would like to see you."

She walked around the bar to hand me my drink and rubbed up against me. In doing so, she made sure her robe opened just enough that I could see a nipple, which I, of course, immediately tongue twirled as she said, "Larry baby, you are a monumental mountain of sex for lustful and love-lorn ladies. I think you should have a couple of really strong drinks because you may get to say hello to Jean Bonner sooner than you think." She gave me a kiss and squeeze-teased my staff surroundings.

Chapter 9
The Return of the "Redsnapper"

(Jean's Back)

I heard a door open and looked up, it was Jean. She was walking towards the staircase that leads down from her room. She began her tantalizing decent by showing no concern for the wave of openings provided for viewing pleasure by her next to nothing see-through nightie. Each sexy downward, sideways, swirl-twist step she took exposed more skin. Soft, silky, skin, that could easily be mentally and visually devoured through the transparency of her lavender lace nightie. I must've looked like I had seen a ghost but I really didn't care.

There was Jean, there was my babysitter, there was my very first sex instructor. There was the keeper of the key for my first real (*Red-Snapper*) introduction. There was my very first true love. She taught my lips to kiss, my tongue to travel, and my cock to come. THERE WAS JEAN!!!

She was barefooted and walking toward me with a motorized sexy-strut-butt-bounce that was surely designed to be a self-serving invitation for an eventual joint replacement. It was screaming, "For your eyes only, Larry." That sexy-strut and personalized butt-bounce pronounced my name louder with each step she took. By the time she got over to where I was standing, I had delivered a double-nut-buster that was running down my leg an about to flood the floor.

I was stutter-speeched. My heart skipped a beat. I think it might even have stopped. I believe the movie (back to the future) had already been thought of and they sent a car to pick me up. For us, time did not stand still, it went backwards. I was still in that puppy- love-status with a heart-hurting hard-on for Jean.

I had no idea how to handle this and I think they must've known that. If the truth were known, they probably planned it. I mean, there was Kristi with a K and an I, and there was Jean, my very first love machine. One had taught me and the other one was taunting me. I very excitedly said, "Jean, I'm having a hard time processing this. It's like I'm going back in time. Are you here to teach me more and continue my training, or are you here to check my progress while my talents you are draining?"

Jean walked over to me. She put one hand on my crotch and the other one behind my head. Then kissed me softly with feelings while squeeze-rolling my Kum-saturated cock-an-balls. She stepped back and said, "Wow, what a warm, wet welcome you have prepared for me, Larry my love. We must appreciate our passion for a fire that still burns."

She dropped immediately to her knees, opened my belt, only to be greeted by a come-crazy-cock. I dropped another load. My love-juices were welcomed by a lustful and long overdue desire for her memories of yesterday to return. I could almost hear her dreaming as those memories were swallowed by her hungry for my love lips, mouth, and throat. She softly performed a sucking serenade of my cock, balls, and entire scrotum area, then said as she stood up and kissed me again. "Well, my dear long-lost Larry love, it appears life has served you largely!

It is so good to see you, Larry. I have missed you so very much. I'm really happy to see and hear you feel the same. I am also extremely happy to hear all the nice compliments Kristi has been paying you. I guess our training days paid off.

After they sent you away to school, I never had another male partner. They were always female. You were my first and you will be the last male lover in my life. Kristi and I are together, and very much in love with each other. I may have taught you lots of things, but you taught me how to love, I thank you for that, Larry.

Although your mother and my mother may not feel the same, I am glad they agreed to let me be your babysitter. I hope nothing I subjected you to or anything we did was damaging to you in any way.

I have lots of deep feelings and so many fond memories of you. I will always love you in my own very special way. I have hoped and dreamed of this day much too long. In a way, I'm sorry it had to happen like it did. Although I am sure Kristi enjoyed her sex shopping spree."

Jean walked out of my arms and into Kristi's. She gave her what I thought might be interpreted as a long-lasting never dying love kiss. Then she said, "Larry, shall we solicit Kristi's comments for complementary comparison?" They both looked at me. I felt as though I were in a daze. My mind was swimming with envy for the kiss Jean had bestowed upon Kristi's lips. She continued, "I am so relieved to finally have loosened my load. Larry, Kristi can tell you how heavy you are because she has carried part of this load with me."

I had no experience in handling things of this magnitude and no idea how to respond. Jean had taught me about sex but not how to analyze the results. I said the first thing that came to my mind. "Before we start comparing anything, I would like to say ditto, double ditto, double-double ditto to everything you just said. And I really do mean everything. Also, nobody told me why I was being sent away to school. I do remember my aunt saying something to my mother about you and me.

I am glad you found someone to love that would help you carry the burden I brought into your life. I could never find anybody to replace you, Jean. I have tried hard to do so, but there was only one Jean. You trained me so well that daily orgasms became a habit. Even if I had to use my own hand with visions of you laying spread-eagle and naked on my bed. Finger painting picture miracles you could work for me with your **red-snapper**. You lay longing and lovely with that look of lusty-love you wore so well, while perfectly positioning your body for the pleasures of my love. A love which you orchestrated and fine-tuned. You had me performing your personal love Symphony and deeply desiring to do so. I wanted the wonders of your pussy's presence as my lips pilfered through the paradise valleys of your always scrumptious **Red Snapper**. Oh yes, my dear Jean, you trained me well. I could never forget you, nor do I want to. I puppy loved you then and I will probably puppy love you always. I don't think I'm damaged, I don't feel damaged. Maybe if you and Kristi are agreeable, we could all get together and examine me for the possibility of being damaged goods.

And lastly, I would like to say that I wish you had never had to worry about any of this. Jesus Christ, I was having the time of my life. Thanks to you, the girls in that private Christian school never knew what hit-em. All my teachers were preachers and their children went to school there. I am sure you know what they say about the preacher's daughter.

Now, if I might suggest, unless it's infringing on anybody's private territory, and especially since you are both dressed for it, why don't we all three partake of some stimulating midnight sex snacks." I lifted my glass for a toast to my proposal. They looked at each other then back at me and lifted their glasses in approval and together they said, "That's what we were hoping for, Larry."

I looked at the clock it was almost 3 A.M. I didn't have to be at work until three in the afternoon. And I knew I would be able to exist on a couple hours sleep. Kristi and Jean did not seem to be too concerned.

Kristi fixed us all another drink and said, "Shall we formulate a plan of action or should we just go with the flow?" Jean replied, "Why don't we let Larry decide." I came back with, "Woah-woah-woah, don't put me in the middle." Kristi looked at me with those sin-filled eyes and asked, "Larry, if you are in a bed with two beautiful young ladies such as Jean and myself, is there any place else in that bed you would rather be than in the middle?" I said, "Point well taken. I guess it's obvious I am not used to threesomes." Jean chimed in with, "These days I believe it's referred to as having a ménage à trois'."

Then she said, "Larry, you have spent a couple of hours making hard fast hurtful love with Kristi, and four years in sex training with me. How much do you trust us? I have spent five years hurting over you and me, and I fully intend to show you just how much love can hurt. Before I am through with you tonight, you will have much more than mental memories of molestation to remind you of me. You must remember that love hurts but true love conquers all and makes everything worthwhile. And so I will say to you, my dear long-lost Larry-love, we cannot wait to get your sex-craved shaft between us and the sheets. I know I can speak for Kristi as well as myself when I say this, we have been, oh, so much looking forward to legally fucking the dog-shit out of you while giving you an education in side by side saddle straddling. Once again, I ask, how much do you trust us?"

I responded with, "Jean, I have always trusted you. I couldn't wait until it was time for you to arrive so you could show me more and we could do things together. You never intentionally hurt me that I can remember, so why shouldn't I trust you now? I wish I could erase all your mental pain. If that is what tonight must be about, then so be it. As far as Kristi, I know she likes pain.

Maybe I'm beginning to realize where some of her need for pleasurable pain comes from. I'm good with whatever happens as long as you promise me you will not hold our past against me after tonight."

She looked at me then she looked over at Kristi and smiled. One kissed me on the left cheek and the other kissed me on the right and Kristi said, "Let's have one more drink and get this party started. Everybody can fix their own drink. Larry, I believe you should probably make yours a little stronger, or maybe even make it a double. It might have to last you a while. Jean and I don't normally stop making love to mix drinks."

I started the conversation while we were making our mental preparations for what turned out to be a painfully pleasuring proposition for all of us. I asked, "How long have y'all known each other?" Jean responded with, "I met Kristi the first day I went to work at the CIA. She worked in the same department I was assigned to.

As soon as I got my high school diploma, my job was guaranteed. I had packed my suitcases the day before. All I had to do was go home say goodbye to mom and I was gone.

When I first met Kristi with a K and an I, I got this really strange feeling in the pit of my stomach. Two days later, we had our first date. I was hot to trot when I got to this area. Damn, Larry, after you left, if it had not been for the vegetable substitutes I would not have had any kind of sex besides self-supplied masturbation tools. Every girl in that damn crazy town was afraid to show their lesbianism aspirations and I didn't want a guy."

Kristi set her glass down and announced very politely, "Excuse me, but I have to pee. Now the way I see it, I either go now or pee on everyone later, and I'm not sure everyone is in tune for a swim in the golden stream." She glanced my way as she was headed for the bathroom. I wasn't sure about that particular stream either.

Jean broke her silence with, "Larry, you look a little concerned. What's the matter, baby? You were always okay with everything I wanted to try. Kristi is only an extension of me. Trust me, you will be in good hands.

You don't have any idea what I have been into since you went away. But it's only been with Kristi, nobody else." I replied with, "Jean, I didn't go away, I was sent away and never told why. Apparently, you know why, please tell me. I would really like to know and I think I deserve to know." She gently placed a finger to my lips and told me she would tell me later and not to worry about it. Then she gave me a quick kiss and said, "Bring your drink and I'll take Kristi's. Let's go to the rec-room. I think Kristi's probably got everything set up by now."

She took me on a little tour of the bathroom and her bedroom. I think she was giving Kristi time to do what she had to do and make all the preparations in the recreation room. Jean led me through the door to her bedroom and turned on the light. It was a very large bedroom with what looked like an extra-large king-size bed. I exclaimed, "Very-very nice. So you perform well enough to deserve the master bedroom." She responded with, "No, it's not like that at all; we both have master bedrooms. When we bought this place, we had it custom made to suit us and made sure everything was the same for both. Follow me, the rec-room is downstairs."

I followed her down a spiral staircase to the rec-room. I began looking around as I was making my way down the stairs. Their rec-room was like having a full basement.

Directly across the room from the staircase I was on was another spiral staircase. Since they had the place custom-built so that everything was the same for both, I figured that one must lead down from Kristi's bedroom.

As I continued looking around, it seemed to be designed for whatever pleasures they decided to partake of at the time. Some of the items I could identify were a pool table, a ping-pong table folded up at one end of the room, and a couple pieces of exercise equipment.

One thing I saw that was becoming very popular was a hot-tub. There was also a round sunken bathtub positioned very close to the hot tub. It had a shower with a rather large shower head mounted in the ceiling.

There was a smaller circle track installed directly above the bathtub for the shower curtain to run on. On the outside of the bathtub curtain run was a much larger tubular track. It was equipped with a curtain run that would encompass both the bathtub and the hot tub. I found out later both curtain runs had individual pull string operated spring-loaded tracks.

Kristi and Jean had really put a lot of thought into the planning for this place. It was like a very top of the line bachelorette pad. Then I remembered they were lovers. Perhaps I should categorize it as a lavish lesbian love nest.

As I stepped onto the rec-room floor, the view of another, much larger bar area caught my eye. I said to Jean, "Hey, baby, why did I have to make my drink so strong? You have another bar down here." She replied, "We try not to use that one. It's kind of what you would consider private stock. You know, for special occasions." I came back with, "We haven't seen each other for almost 6 years and that's not special?" She looked over at me with a sexy sultry smile and slap-rolled my entire scrotum area, then administering a soft rolling nut squeeze and very snappishly snapped, "Don't give me a hard time, I want your hard-on. I am your sex instructor, not your babysitter. Would you rather create a bedtime story or have me read you one," while she kept applying the same squeeze roll procedure on my nut sack.

This was a part of Jean I did not know. Maybe the 5 ½ years had taken its toll. We continued walking as she showed me different fixtures and explained their standings in the rec-room.

There was also a half bath, or what some people might consider a powder room. Its door was mounted flush with the back wall and opened to the inside for reasons that became obvious to me later in life. Their entire condo seemed to personify the enormous amount of planning that had been put into play to satisfy the term, wisest, and best use of space.

Suddenly, Kristi appeared, displaying her nudity and beautifully proportioned body parts. She was just stepping off the staircase and started walking towards the bathtub. When I looked around to ask Jean what was going on, she had dropped her nightie and was sharing her gifts of nature's niceties as well. She never said a word, just started walking towards the bathtub displaying that little sexy-strut butt-bounce. After that night, I referred to it as her stiff-tongue and hard-on strut.

Here I was fully clad including my shoes and socks. Bound and determined not to be left behind, I started discarding articles of clothing on my way to the tub. By the time I reached nudity and the tub, they were both submerged and covered with bubbles.

Jean looked over at Kristi and said, "Honey, what you see is why I prefer women. Men are always walking around with a stiff-dick and dropping their clothes everywhere." Kristi came back with, "But doesn't it look tasty? Wouldn't you just love to chomp down on that, chew it up and swallow it balls and all?"

Knowing something was about to happen that I did not want to miss out on, I was very quick to retrieve my clothes. I folded and laid them in a nice neat pile right beside Jean's nightie. Then I headed back to the tub, exhibiting a fully charged prick, a tight nut sack, and a tongue that couldn't talk and didn't want to.

It's a good thing the tub was a little larger than a normal bathtub because as I started to sit down and slide in the tub, Kristi grabbed my cock and pulled me in. She began sucking my cock underwater and I headed straight for Jean's titty's. Her tits were nice and firm. A little on the smaller side, not much more than a mouthful, which meant you didn't have to chase them.

Kristi's head was bobbing in and out of the water to catch her breath. She made sure to maintain possession of my cock while at the same time providing a trolling procedure of my main vein with her lower lip and teeth.

Jean had sprung into action by preparing both of Kristi's nipples for sample sucking, while at the same time massaging her pussy with an open hand. She was also allowing an occasional single-digit finger-fuck to take place from whatever hand Kristi had available.

I was swallowing bubbles. Bubbles are going up my nose and probably coming out my eyes. I finally worked my way down Jean's tummy from her tits to my old training grounds. It was the home of her *RED-SNAPPER*.

There was a sudden sense of satisfaction, or maybe I should say security, as my mouth and lips began to masterfully massage her once upon a time very familiar pussy. I felt so at home I wanted to climb inside and never leave again. Suddenly, I became ambushed by the desire to make Jean orgasmically proud of her pupil.

While we were all struggling to keep our mouths and edible body parts close to the surface, Jean decided to have a little loving mouth-to-mouth tongue-travel with Kristi. This meant my shaft became available for the insertion of other bodily orifices.

Kristi didn't waste any time, I knew what she wanted and liked. She kept total control of mouth-to-mouth and tongue to tonsil with Jean while grabbing my cock with one hand and pushing it in the direction of her pussy. That didn't last long, only a couple pussy pumps before sliding it back enough to take aim on her anal opening.

I was surprised to find that while the two of them remained kiss-connected, Jean was able to position one hand on one cheek and the other hand on the other cheek of Kristi's ass. She was providing the anal opening spread on Kristi's butt for a less painful entrance of my cock because she knew what Kristi wanted.

Kristi positioned my prick perfectly for prune puncturing, then she gave a little tug on my nut sack. I bit down tightly on Jean's pussy and teasingly tongued her clit, simultaneously giving it a serious nibble-nip, pushing my face hard into her pussy for leverage, and slamming my shaft deep inside Kristi's under-water back-door-split-open-hole. I knew some water had to be seeping into Kristi's annual cavity. I could feel it following my prick and I wasn't sure if that was such a good idea or not. One thing I had learned by this time about playing love games was that sooner or later the answer to whether things were good ideas or not would surface.

Well, guess what, I don't know if anybody had an orgasm but I do know everybody choked and swallowed bubbles. Kristi screamed and threw her arms around Jean's shoulders so tight I thought she was going to squeeze her in-two. I was trying to take a breath, eat Jeans pussy, and pump a prune, without swallowing water or allowing too many bubbles the pleasure of raping my nostrils.

On one of my trips to the surface for air, I realized someone had turned on the shower. They had also activated the shower curtain around the bathtub. I knew it had to be Jean but I wasn't sure why so I asked her. She told me she was worried because I seemed to be having too much fun bouncing around in and out and under the water and was afraid I might get hurt or drowned.

Then she said, "I could never live that down. I can just hear all those loose tongue's waggin' back in that dumb ass town. She trained him for a sex toy when he was a boy so she could fuck him to death when he grew up." Then Jean smiled and handed me a towel with one hand, and with the other grabbed my pecker and gave it a couple quick gentle jerks to let me know it was time to get out of the tub.

Chapter 10
"Lost Love-Alone At Last"

As we were drying off, she started walking towards the bar. I, of course, followed her since that was one of my favorite places to be. We had dried off and wiped the bubbles away and were sitting naked on the barstools. I noticed Kristi was nowhere around. I asked her, "What happened to Kristi?" She replied, "She told me she was feeling a little tired and thought she might get some rest. I think you wore her out earlier last night."

I wasn't buying that. Kristi seemed to me to be very deeply determined to have as much sex of any kind that time would allow. She was a damn good fucking machine and I knew she could fuck me to death anytime she felt like It. Her exiting the scene happened so quickly it must have been planned so Jean and I could share some quality downtime.

I said to her, "So, Jeannie baby, it's just you and me for the rest of the night. Is this a special enough of an occasion for a drink?" Jean came back with, "No-one calls me Jeannie, it insinuates a much looser personality than I like to project. But it's okay if you call me Jeannie; I think you've earned that right. In answer to your question, you're damn right it is special enough, Larry. It is special enough for several drinks. And we're going to have them.

This time they're going to say that she took him down to DC got him drunk and fucked him. I hope you like champagne because that's what this special occasion is deserving of. I finally have you here with me. Nobody can ship you away this time. You will have to be the one to make the decision to stay or go."

I was really not a connoisseur of champagne, mainly because where I came from they couldn't spell it, buy it, or pronounce it, much less drink it. But I was ready and willing to find out all the many different doors of dominance champagne could open for lovemaking.

Since I have been permitted to call Jean (Jeannie), and since I prefer to call her Jeannie, I shall refer to her as Jeannie from this day forward. Thank you very much!!! She has truly been my Jeannie with a bottle and a bedroom.

Jeannie had prepared the serving stand with a bottle of champagne in a bucket of ice, two champagne glasses, and a couple of hand towels. She started rolling the stand towards the hot tub and motioned for me to follow her. Then she said, "I think this will be a more relaxing place for comfortable conversation."

She opened the campaign and poured each glass about half full. She touched her glass to my glass and proposed a toast as she said to me, "Here is to you and me, our past and our future." She lifted her glass and touched my glass again to seal the toast. Then with her voice slightly above a whisper, she said, "Let's do it this way." Jeannie directed my first sip from her glass and hers from mine. The automatic follow-up was hooking around and through each other's arms drinking from our own glasses.

The funny part about this was that during the entire toasting process, our eyes were stuck like glue to each other. My mind was kind of in limbo and I felt like I was in la-la land. I guess I wasn't expecting all that. It felt like I just got married or engaged.

I turned around and Jeannie had already stepped down into the hot tub carrying her drink with her. Being as accommodating as I possibly could under the circumstances, I followed her. And I asked her, "What was that all about?" She replied, "Oh, I don't know, it felt good. You have the most gorgeous eyes, I can see deep into your soul. You know, of course, the eyes are the windows of the soul." Still, in a semi-stable state of mind, I responded, "You have very pretty eyes also, however, I think they hypnotized me because I don't believe I saw your soul. My dear Jeannie, are you a hypnotist or a witch? It seems I remain spellbound after all these years. Please, take me and do with me as you wish."

Jeannie had finished her drink and I asked her if she would like another. She shook her head yes and handed me her glass. I finished mine and poured us both another glass of champagne.

Once again, we were seated side-by-side in the nice warm bubbling water of the hot tub.

Jeannie started in on a conversation about our past. She began with, "I know I promised I would tell you about what happened. I am going to make it as short and painless as possible. I do not want it to ruin our mood. I happen to like you in this mood with me."

She continued, "One day, while you were busy achieving perhaps the highest score I could have given you for performing your favorite act of sex, I noticed the door to the bedroom we were using for your training exercises was open slightly.

Your aunt was standing there watching us. You could not have seen her because of the position you were in. She left without saying a word. I knew she would tell both our mothers and I was going to be in lots of trouble.

I guess I really didn't care. I know I was so proud of how far you had come in learning your art. You were the best little Cunt-Licker, and the control you displayed in whether to bring me the pleasure of an early climax or doubling that pleasure by diligently dragging me into a star-burst explosion of several mini-orgasms... You were amazing for your age. I remember thinking, *it feels so good, I'm just going to lay here and let him finish.*

I didn't say anything to you about your aunt being there because I knew the whole thing was my fault and I should be the one to get punished. I had no idea they were going to send you away to school. I don't suppose there would have been anything I could have done even if I had known.

Your family and my mother decided they wanted to keep it as quiet as possible and it would be best with you out of the picture. My mother volunteered to pay your tuition for two years at the private school. Lots of people wondered about things but they managed to keep it fairly quiet.

My mother made me get a job so I could help pay for my mistake. She didn't trust me babysitting anymore so I had to get a job at the drugstore soda fountain. There I would be under the watchful eye of the nosy public at all times while performing my duties as a soda-jerk.

Incidentally, that is where my first lesbian affair was birthed. You would know her if I told you her name. It serves no purpose to take that road so we'll just let it rest.

In closing this conversation. let's just say, **I was wrong and taught you to play. They sent you away but you still played. I had to get a job so I could pay, for having so much fun teaching you to play.**

And now, dear Larry, what I wish to do with you will come with your consent. Please let this be the last time we speak of our past. Let us lay those memories to rest and work on making new and better ones for future reference.

I love you, Larry, in a way I don't understand. I know there will always be a place for you and our love deep inside my heart. There are so many different types of love, and ways to love someone. I know our love will always be special and have that feel-good feeling, with memories in our days of **"Aftergolw"**. Now, at your request, I will take you and do with you as I wish!!!"

((And so it was!!!))

After a short conversation in the hot tub explaining some puzzles of the past, she took me and did with me as she wished. No way was I in control. I was like putty in Jeannie's magic hands, or clay she was molding for the manipulation of my mind as well as forming my body for her own pleasures and desires. I was truly hypnotic when she was present. She must have been some sort of a witch. If so, she was casting a spell that I ever so much enjoyed being under. **Jeannie, Jeannie, Jeannie, I thank you so very much for that part of my life!!!**

Now, we were both ready for another drink. Whoops, that was the end of that bottle. Jeannie noticed the bottle was empty and she said, "Go over to the bar and get one of the bottles on the right-hand side of the second shelf. It's the best there is for body washing and it gives you a better buzz. Have you ever had Dom Perignon?" She handed me a glass and I responded with, "I don't think so but I doubt it. I'm not really into champagne, I'm more of a beer kind of person." With the look of a sensual predatory temptress on her face, Jeannie came back with, "You might need it, it'll keep you from getting lost in the bedroom, and creates all kinds of new places for you to go. It will help you climb mountains and teach you to swim rivers. It will lead you through the many valleys of lust that lovemaking might burden you with throughout life. Champagne is food for a love makers brain."

Chapter 11
"Inside The Walls Of Afterglow"

I guess we were in what you would call preparation stages for a lovers liaison. Although Jeannie had said no plans had been made ahead of time, it seemed like everything was just too readily available to be inconspicuous.

We were both still working on our third glass of champagne. With the encouragement of the warm water in the hot tub, the champagne was starting to take effect. I had set my drink on the shelf that runs around the top of the hot tub and was busying my lips and hands on Jeannie's warm, wet, extremities. All of a sudden, Jeannie set her drink up on the same shelf and started coveting my body. She began with a fast forceful kiss that almost extracted my tongue while simultaneously administering an underwater ball bouncing cock jerk.

The energy from it all brought us to an underwater warm familiar number **(69'er).** My pleasures were interrupted every few seconds by finding it necessary to come up for air. I noticed the warm water added a very heavy scrumptious secretion flavor-charge to Jeannie's pussy produced love-lava. My already self-induced salivating senses had fallen victim to the uncontrollably demanding desires for the taste of temptation. **The afterglow** of Jeannie's hot, sweet little pussy, **My Red Snapper of yesteryear.** I had entered a different galaxy. One of the memories that were filled with, and produced an even greater love-hungry lust, accompanied by spontaneously explosive, orgasmically satisfying demands and desires for pleasured pussy contentment. It was like the same process of how warming honey puts more emphasis to the flavor except it had been magnified 10,000 times. I had found my own little corner of her pussy planet heaven and chose to stay there even if it meant drowning.

The warm water pussy flavor had placed a permanent demand in my mind. I went up for air several times only to return again and again having run out of breath. In my mind, I'm thinking I must find a way to preserve and bring permanence to that warm water pussy flavor.

The underwater (69'er) was very interesting but tiresome. After a couple of nostrils fill with water and a choke or two later, the sexual excitement kind of started to dwindle. You might say the desire to molest your mate on dry-land became prevalent for both of us.

It seemed like ever since we sealed the toast we were doing everything with a lot more togetherness. I stayed behind and helped Jeannie out of the hot tub with a gentle little hand squashing butt boost. She reciprocated by taking one hand and pulling until I was far enough out she could grab my cock and balls with both hands. That move persuaded me to be rather helpful in assisting her desires to operate on dry-land.

Together we visited the linen closet where we quickly gathered enough pillows and towels to turn one of the large workout mats into a king-size bed. Miraculously, the sheets fit the rather large mat perfectly. I wondered why Jeannie didn't fuck around with men. Surely this isn't Jeannie and Kristi's playpen, if so maybe I'll be lucky enough to join them sometime.

Just as though she could read my mind, Jeannie said in a rather unusually rough tone, "Larry, you better bring your sweet ass back to earth boy! I know I said let's think about the future. Mine and your future is right here right now. You have to make me happy here before you can go any farther into dreamland. So bring your ass and the rest of that fucking lovemaking machine that I created over here and lay it down. It's time for you to pay your dues. They say payback is hell.

I know you think I'm a witch. Now I have a little magic I'm going to work on you. I'm going to take you to heaven before I put you through hell. So lay down, baby, spread your arms out above your head and spread your legs to either side of the mat. You have a choice, you can close your eyes or I'll supply you with a blindfold.

Everything that happens in the next hour or so will be a surprise. You will not be able to see any of it as it is happening. There are a couple more old sayings that come to mind at this time. One of them is, 'What you can't see can't hurt you.' And of course, the other one is, 'You never see the one that hit you.'"

My "God," that damn woman talks a lot. I kept wanting to say, shut the fuck up and hit me with a piece of your pussy. Fuck me, baby. She was still talking to me in the background while she fitted me with a blindfold and gave me a little sip of champagne. I asked her for more and she said, "Sure, baby, you can have as much as you want because you're probably going to need it."

I wanted to say something so I finally said, "Jeannie honey, you have been talking a lot. I know your throat must be sore, and it might make your tonsils swell. Maybe you should put your lips to better use and wrap them around something that can lubricate your tonsils. You know, give your throat a soft soothing satisfied feeling with a cover coating of come. In other words, shut the fuck up, baby, just suck my cock and bring your Red-Snapper home to "daddy" so I can continue my dinner in your diner. Nothing could taste finer than lunch from Jeannie's warm vagina. I've got the hungry's for your love, darlin', we can talk later." She interrupted me with, "You'd really like that, wouldn't you? It will happen soon enough."

Jeannie continued with, "The only reason I'm talking so much is that I have a lot of pent-up emotions concerning you. Almost five years of backed up verbal frustration brought about by the lack of orgasmic bliss provided by our earlier life's love creation." I interrupted her and said, "For Christ's sake, Jeannie, will you just relax. Please let me help you put an end to your frustrations. I've got what you need and you know it, baby. Just place your pretty little luscious perplexed pussy right here on the lips you taught to satisfy it. **UEEW-EE BABY,** sit on my face and make-your-self-heavy. I will eat your pussy for the next five years for payback. By the time I take my face out of your snatch-patch, it will be so swollen it won't fit under the 14th St., Bridge."

The next thing I know, in a matter of a split-second, she had slipped something over my hands that felt like a rope. She wrapped it around my wrists and was pulling my hands, angling them out from my head and up from my shoulders. She must've tied them to something because I couldn't pull either toward my head or down to my side.

I wasn't sure what the hell was going on. I'm not even sure why I trust her. I haven't seen her for almost 5 years and she obviously has been staying in touch with people that know me or knew where I was. That type of behavior would almost fall under the category of stalking.

Just then another cliché popped into my miseried mind: Hell hath no fury like a woman scorned. I didn't believe that I had caused her to be scorned, or shamed. But who knows what's running through her mind. I guess I'll find out soon enough… if I live.

Kristi had to know where I was working. There is no way she just happened to drop by and we met by chance. That was all preplanned by Jeannie. Hell, I wouldn't be surprised if she didn't fuck the owner of that novelty shop and talk him into giving me a job. She lives almost right around the corner from the damn store.

I bet you a damn dollar she had a hand in that. With Kristi helping her, both of them probably fucked him silly. As much as Kristi likes pain and Jeannie likes to talk, I'm surprised he didn't give them the damn store just to get rid of-em.

All these thoughts were running through my head in a matter of a minute. Uh-oh, there goes my feet. The noose just tightened around my ankles and now I'm being stretched out in a position to be drawn and quartered. Oh shit, I wonder if that's what she's got in mind. I hope not.

I don't know what the hell I'm worried about. I was nine years old when Jean first started training me. And she spent the next four years being nice and gentle, kind and caring, seductive and perverted.

No, I don't mean that. I know some people might think that way but I don't. I probably was to blame for more of the sex training than she was. I mean, after all, I wanted it to happen. I know I was only nine years old when it started but I had been chasing little split-tails all my life to that point.

It must have become obvious to me that what I was chasing could not satisfy my desires. So, I was happy to have fallen into a Jeannie-seduction-connection.

Oh shit, what the hell is that noise? It sounds like a little motor, hope it's not a saw. It feels like something is being poured or sprinkled on me. It's on my face too. It tastes like champagne, so that must be what it is. That motor noise is getting closer. What is that other noise? Sounds like a gushy spray, maybe it was whipped cream. She just sprayed some in my armpits, it feels cool. I'll bet it's a cool whip or whipped cream.

If that the case, o-oh-yeah, she just sprayed around my cock and packed my nut-sack. Now she's going up the crack of my ass with whatever it is. Here comes the noise again and it is getting closer. Oh shit, what is it? It's tipping my skin. Now it's feather-tipping around my shaft like 500 little pen-pricks a second. I can feel the tailwind it creates as it travels all around and up and down my love muscle. Now she's tip-pricking the rim around the head of my cock with it. I wish she'd suck the damn thing. I'd like to run it all away down her esophagus to her breast bone, maybe that would pay her back for some of this crazy shit she's doing.

The motor sounds like a drill. If it is a drill I wonder what she's got in it. Could be a feather or a small whip of some sort? I do know it is certainly not a drill bit. It definitely creates a weird sensation on my nipples and the head of my cock. I noticed she was not getting close to my balls, or for that matter, anywhere there is hair. It must be because it could easily get tangled in the hair.

I will say it feels good and adds excitement to the presentation. However, there are certain places it feels better. One of them is the part of my ass crack that connects the bottom of my ball-bag to my ass-hole. It definitely feels good and supplies a tiny-turn-on when she is tickle-walking it on and around my anal-opening. Hopefully, she'll stay with the pen-pricking-tickling-pleasures instead of prune-puncturing. Ouch, I bet that would make the "ole" butt-crack-tighten-up.

I guess the next hour or so I'm going to be thinking to myself or trying to deduce what is happening to me. I'll try to make it as exciting for you to read, as it was for me to have happened.

This particular toy must give her a feeling of power over her partner. To say the least, it's interesting and causes one to give a lot of thought to the fact that you are somewhat voluntarily playing the part of a sex guinea pig, trying to find out what tool of the trade is best suited for pleasure. Or quite possibly which one would present the most pleasurable pain. This one so far, even though I don't know exactly what it is, possesses both pleasure and pain.

The pain is mostly mental because you don't know what to expect. But the traveling tailwind of the tiptoeing prickler as its journey takes it from the tips of your fingers to the tips of your toes, and especially the ball of your foot, creates a rather gentle type of soothing massage.

Uh-oh, something new. Now I know it's Cool Whip. She just covered my nose and gave me a mustache and a beard. She must've got rid of the motorized pecker-prickler I can't hear it anymore. Thank "God" for that, I got kinda tired of guessing what it was.

Then, kind of whispering, Jeannie said, "Open your mouth, Larry, and I'll put a little dash-of-Dom on your tongue." As I opened my mouth, I said, "The lady speaks," as I felt four quick squirts of champagne saturate my tongue and the interior of my mouth. She apparently had the champagne in a smaller spray bottle.

The next thing I know she had quickly saturated my pecker with champagne and pleasured it with Cool Whip. I was hoping I knew the next step, and I was right. This was a fun time to have the blindfold on. I pretty much knew what was going on.

As she was lip and tongue teasing the tip of her long-lost toy, I heard a few quick sprays of champagne and one big fizzy spray of Cool Whip. That must've been on her because it wasn't on me. Actually, it was in her pussy. I could tell because she started force-feeding my joint into her mouth all around her jaws and down her throat. She gifted me with a surprise landing that could have been fatal for me. Instead, she provided me with the most delicious dose of delirium in the form of a fur burger from heaven. She had sprayed champagne in her pussy and filled it full of Cool Whip. Then sprayed champagne in my mouth and covered my nose and chin with Cool Whip. I wish my hands were free so I could pull myself all the way into that perfect piece of prime pussy.

The taste was great, I could tell I was getting a few pussy hairs. I am sure she was having my pubic hairs also in the process of performing this slush-fest (69)'er. I wonder who can eat the most cock and balls or pussy and ass-holes. ***"I believe I shall have mine with Cool Whip and Dom Perignon, along with a side order of pubic hairs if you please. Thank you very much, my dear Jeannie.!!!"***

This is the kind of lovemaking session that drives one crazy. Your hands and feet are tied and you can't move. She can jam as much pussy up to your nostrils and pack them with Cool Whip as she wishes. Hell, she could jam whatever she wants wherever she wants to and you can't do a damn thing about it. When you try to breathe, you get a drink of champagne mixed with Cool Whip along with whatever bodily orifice or body part has presented itself to your mouth at the time.

The sex guessing game does keep your attention. As long as you can keep your mind on what's not going on you can eliminate all surprises. You know that sooner or later whatever is not going on will happen. I must say, the ass and ball lip-suction cleaning procedure Jeannie provided me with was intensely pleasurable.

In the next couple of minutes, she took that split-open-hole between her legs on a trip over every inch of my body, including my nose, forehead, and my hair. I think I had Cool Whip packed in my ears, which may be the reason I can barely hear out of my right ear now, but that would not stop me from doing it all over again if the opportunity presented itself.

Every now and then, she would reach over and get that little spray bottle of champagne and spray it all over my body. Then she rubbed it all up and down into my toes and back up over where she had been pussy trailing, then take a slow-moving hand-tracking of my ass and give my prune a slightly penetrated punch-plug squirt of Dom-Perignon.

I don't know how many times I got my rocks. I knew she was swallowing mine. Her love juices were being mixed with my fur-burger fixens and finally spread on what she was planning on having for lunch - the whole of me.

She was sitting on my stomach when she reached up and took off the blindfold. She had made such a great effort of spreading everything all over me she succeeded in totally covering herself as well as titty's, nipples, hair, and everywhere.

I raised my head a little so I could see what everything looked like. It looked pretty fucking sexy. I started trying to pull everything loose. I wanted to grab on and just devour her. Damn-it, I wanted to eat me some "Jeannie-meat".

As she kind of wrote her name with her finger on my chest, Jeannie said, "I have been planning this for a long time and I thought you might enjoy watching (us)." I'm wondering, who is us, me and her or her and Kristi? I asked very curiously, "Eh--who is us?"

She suddenly started unfolding this rather large room divider that she had put in place while I was blindfolded. When she finished the unfolding it surrounded the whole work-out mat. Each section was equipped with a tilt adjustment either up or down. She adjusted the top parts to a slight downward tilt. Then she said, "What do you mean who is us?" As she very carefully uncovered each panel it became obvious they were all mirrors. She looked over at me and inquired once more, "Who did you think (us) was going to be?" I admittedly replied, "I wasn't sure, and I am honestly still not sure the way things have been happening. I kind of thought it might be that you and Kristi were going to perform some sort of sadistic or cannibalistic act of sex with my body. You will have to admit you have made me look quite edible."

Jeannie had already started partaking of the forbidden fruit and was about to plant more when she looked at me very seriously and said, "Let me make this perfectly clear for the last time, Larry. I was hoping you would understand but apparently you don't. As long as you are within these walls, **we are taking a trip back in time and you are mine!!!**

You may not have realized this so try to understand what I am saying to you. Kristi is my lover and my friend. She is also my roommate and co-owner of this condo. She did me a very big favor last night by tracking you down and bringing you home. And from what she told me, she received a rather sizable reward for doing so. As a matter of fact, Kristi got much more of you last night than I ever wanted her to have. I know what she likes, and she told me how well you treated her. Kristi knows how I feel and now I hope you understand how I feel.

When I found out you were coming to this area, I went to a lot of trouble and expense to find out where you were going to be living and where you were going to be working. So, Larry baby, I want you to try to understand when I say to you that when it comes to Kristi, for you, Kristi is off-limits. And when it comes to you, for Kristi, you are off-limits. Unless it is something that has been planned and discussed by the three of us."

I glanced up and around to the mirrors. I looked like a runny mess of a man whose pecker had gone soft on him. It's wasn't worthy of being referred to as a cock so I just called it a pecker.

How the hell could you, if you were a cock, explain going soft when you have a sex-filled environment? Especially when a sex-crazed nude woman possessing the mind-set of a wanton in love was laying claim to your lower torso. It was certainly nothing I could comprehend. I had a violent desire to slap or pound it until hardness was achieved. Instead, I was forced to endure the embarrassment of owning a limp-dick through a sadistically sick and sexy situation of a lust-filled lady laying claim to my love muscle by controlling a lazy lovemaking liaison.

I guess it was just because of the conversation we had been having, especially the part that Kristi and I were off-limits for each other. I never did like that kinda shit. Something I got from my dad was stubbornness. Just as sure as she tells me I'm not going to do something or I cannot do something, she can bet her warm, wet, and wonderfully flavored pussy juice that I am going to do it or die trying.

Jeannie had started to repair and replace the perpendicularity of my shaft by covering the whole of my nut sack with champagne and Cool Whip. Saturated and sticky, though, it may have been. Using both hands, she applied a push-pull jerk-off level masturbation process to put more emphasis on successfully persuading it to up-right status. A position much preferred to that of the horribly half-assed horizontal hard-on it had become victimized by.

She looked up at me and said, "I guess I caused this, but I can fix it, watch this." I did so without responding to her previous comments. I was watching her work her slippery cunt-lips up, down, and around my shinning champagne saturated shinbone. The mirrors were great; I could see her split-open-hole spreading wider and wider as she slowly slid down my leg. I watched her masterfully maneuver my ankle with a pussy-lip-walking procedure and she didn't stop there. Jeannie took her twat right on down and gave my toes a little taste of something sweet. She spent the next half-hour or so performing an open-faced pussy-lip body surfing procedure. She cunt-fucked my entire body.

In my days of after-glow, I shall always revel in a mental memory picture of her shin-fucking process. That gave birth to the sexy appearance of a titillatingly tantalizing spread-open pussy-lip suction-cup procedure she performed, while serving up a love-juice mixture for an appetizer on both my nipples. Then she brought to life the eternal memory of her dominant force. **Jeannie's Red Snapper in full magnetic charge** blazed her tauntress trail of temptation around my nose, mouth, and lips. She finally made a love-lava-landing for a taste test to my tongue. Then she provided permanent placement of her warm, wet, weeping, with champagne and Cool Whip pussy-lips. "Memories that shall live forever within my walls of **afterglow!!!**"

With her lips around the head of my shaft and her teeth hooking under the rim a little, she gave a few fast strokes and a teasingly soft bite or two. I could feel it starting to reclaim its former firmness and I said, "The mirrors provided a perfect view of your sensational-shin-sex and nipple massaging. Turn it around baby and lay it on my chin. I want to watch myself disappear into your champagne and Cool Whip covered snatch-patch while I eat my way to your perfectly furnished with flavor pussy parlor."

My love muscle had regained full hardness again and Jeannie was playing a perfect part by positioning her pussy in the mirrors for my viewing pleasure. And what a pleasure it was. As soon as it came into view, I shot a stream that glanced off the end of her nose and onto her cheekbone as she was about to lay a lip-lock on the head of my prick. She took her fingers and wiped it toward her lips and went on kiss-caressing my cock as though nothing had happened. I could feel a warm round-up of rapid-fire-jizzum climbing up the main vein of my shaft, there it would lay claim to the outpouring of another orgasmic explosion.

I was watching the mirrors so that I could teasingly touch the tip of my tongue to her twat and watch her shiver from above. Jeannie knew what I was waiting for. I thought that was what she wanted also. As she started to turn her body around, she began performing a sensual pussy lip to body sex dance.

Jeannie knew what her body moves were doing to my mind. She finger walkingly trailed both our bodies with rhythm while tauntingly twisting nipples and pinching tits. Her pussy almost touched my lips and I thought she was going to set on my face. Then she very quickly pulled the "ole" switcheroo by punishing my body with a double circle of tit slapping and pussy lip massaging, then returning to our 69'er. When it happened, the picture projected by the mirrors was so intensely effective the Old-Jizzum-Trail blew its flood gates. I simultaneously buried my mouth in her pussy and my nose in her ass as I plunged my shaft deep into her esophagus. Jeannie made sure that each rib of her talented throat provided the maximum sensation from her rolling rib-rub on the rim around the head of my cock. She knew exactly what she was doing. This is what she wanted all the time. She was only trying to build the excitement while overflowing my ramrod.

She choked a little as a result of her prick pleasuring. I mumbled, "Yeah, baby, I guess you caused that, too." The choking created more excitement, which brought on another Jizzum-Trail eruption, followed by a Jeannie double-choke.

I followed the mirrors with my eyes from where it showed my mouth and her pussy all the way down around the slippery side as it projected her mouth swallowing my cock and balls. I continued my journey of the mirrors up the other side of slipperiness, pausing slightly to tit-watch. Her rolling up and down mouth motion on my prick allowed her titty-nipples to tiptoe gently on my lower torso.

Then, on to the finale of displaying the other side of my pussy-eating jaw-motion. I was salivating savagely, having succumbed to the surrounding slobbers that had secreted from that little split-open-hole between her legs. She was a true **Split-Tail.**

Trying hard not to appear breathless, I moved my head slightly and rolled my eyes up to get a full view as I covered all the mirrors. The shiny appearance provided by the champagne was helping the white of the whipped cream bring flavor and color to the lavender sheet in the background. What a picture; if this could only be captured on canvas, it would make a magnificent mural for my **WALLS OF AFTERGLOW.**

The view brought another dripping drool to my Jeannie's favorite tool, which she tenderly tongued as she turned to me and said, "Are you ready for heaven, Larry? Heaven is ready for you!"

With that, Jeannie turned and reached for the whipped cream. She began to apply it in some kind of orderly fashion, I guess only in her mind. She drew an up-side-down cool whip "U" under my chin and down each side of my esophagus. Then Jeannie trailed the upside-down "U" with the opening ends to each of my nipples and attached them with a whipped cream circle. Jeannie was displaying her artistic ability making it appear as a horseshoe tied to two pegs.

I remember wondering what she was thinking as she drew a circle around my chicken breast, as they call it. Then she filled it with champagne. She sprayed a mist of champagne over all of her drawings and my entire upper torso, including my face. There was no analyzing this. **It had to be the results of a good love at a bad time with a good time had by all, still harboring so much pain and suffering yet to fall, it makes the grade of "worthy" to be a Muriel on my wall.** Jeannie was portraying her life over the past five years on my bare body with a cool whip and champagne picture of her heart and soul. **Jeannie was truly MY HEARTS FAVORITE RED-SNAPPING-SPLIT-TAIL.**

Jeannie gave me a drink and said, "I hope you will enjoy this as much as I enjoy doing it for you. I have had many dreams in the past five years of tongue washing your entire body, much like I used to do when we were younger and falling in love with love games. Except this time, you are my love prisoner and I will use champagne and cool whip. I quite possibly could become rather tipsy by the duration of my tender touching and titillating transformation of your tantalizingly-torturing-taunts from the past. As a matter of fact, I hope I do. I know I would find it less painful if it were so.

When this little part of your heaven is completed, you should surely know you have been on my mind every second of the entire time we've been apart. If you have any questions please ask them now. I do not wish to be interrupted. I want to make absolutely sure you enjoy your time spent here as much as possible because hell lies just around the corner. I Love you, Larry!"

I still say she talks too damn much. Maybe it comes from dreaming or being alone too long. I just hope she unties me before she starts putting me through hell. I'd like to be able to mount some sort of defense if I need one.

For the next couple of minutes, she was busy tracing the exterior limit lines for the first part of my body wash with her tongue. They ran from my hairline to about halfway down my sides and squared off just above my bellybutton.

Once she had the limit lines established, the cool whip and champagne containers returned to the scene for a few quick squirts. First was to refresh the cool whip, then to spray a light mist of champagne once again over that same body area. The champagne was kinda like sweat drops lying here and there on my body. My hair was totally wet with champagne, but I don't think she intended to lick the champagne out of my hair. I don't know, maybe so, I guess we'll see.

Once the tongue washing started, it seemed to be working in kind of like, "okay I'll finish one area and then move to the next." She tongue washed my entire four head then sprayed another mist on and licked it off. My opinion on that was so she could get a good amount of champagne to start this procedure with. She did every part of my face.

Jeannie titillatingly tongue massaged my ears, my inner lip and outer lip, my eyebrows, eye-sockets, and nose. I enjoyed the ear-job most, as they were sensitive. If she would just suck and tongue-travel my ears long enough I could probably get a boner. She covered every inch under my chin and around my neck. Jeannie paid individual attention to each rib of my esophagus with her tongue, then she slipped slowly to my underarms. Making sure to share equal time, she traced her tongue frantically across the top of my chest, nipple-nipping on the way.

Her taste-test was a mixture of champagne and cool whip, topped with tongue-swirled armpit-sweat, which she seemed to be starvingly ravishing to extinction. It put an orgasmic glow in her eyes and an extra special move to her motor muscle.

I love armpits. I like to fuck'em too. It's kinda like that little pocket in there is a come-holder. They are sexy as long as the little hair follicles are not too stubby from being shaved. I really don't like the idea of possessing a pin-hole-punctured-prick.

I had a lady friend, back when I was putting all the pieces of split- tails and making love together, that would tell me, "I will suck your dick for 30 minutes if you jack-off in both my armpits and rub it in. Then take the left over come and massage my titty's with it." While I was saturating her armpits and tits, she was masturbating.

??- oh well, everybody's got to be somewhere-??

Well shit, here I go again, off on another tantrum of a tale of two titty's and armpits that should be left for another book. But she was a real sexy lady. I believe she could have had an orgasm while sucking her own toe. I know she could while sucking mine.

You might want to disregard this little rant and wait for that particular book to come out so you get to know the whole story.

Right now, the only thing you need to know is when you are writing memoirs and going through papers and tapes while you're writing them down, you remember certain situations that remind you of others. And you almost feel obligated to document them before you die. Not knowing for sure when you're going to expire your documentation will usually occur when they visit your memory.

Jeannie had reached behind her and was handily slipp-rolling my foreskin with a pinch-pull procedure on my prick, still maintaining position and continuing the slurping-suction of my armpit serenade. I could feel dribbles of wetness from her pussy as she teasingly twisted her twat on my torso. With each twisting move, she positioned her hole a little closer to my pole which was very fast becoming a watering hose for her love nest.

I wish I hadn't been held captive. Jeannie had started a fire and wasn't trying to keep it under control. She just kept adding fuel to the flame. If I were loose she would be in trouble right now. If-if-if another one of those good old country clichés come to mind. If a toad had wings he wouldn't bump his ass on the ground when he jumps. I know I'm tied down but I swear to Christ if I could just get hold of her I would, as Kristi so eloquently puts it, "fuck the dog-shit out of her." That particular phrase must absolutely be referred to from here-to-fore as a coined by Kristi "Quote".

As though Jeannie knew what I was thinking, she took the head of my cock in her hand and rough-rolled it with her palm and fingers. And with a tight grip and a hard wrist snap, twisted my cock a little and pulled down hard. She pulled the right trigger that time. I fired off a strong around but she wasn't expecting it. She tried to move quickly to catch some in her mouth but instead got the "ole" jizzum saturated forehead. Jeannie started speed jerking my prick. She had scraped up some of my last load with her fingers and mixed it with her own dribbles. She licked it off but obviously wanted more. Then she slipped back into her armpit switch-hitting lick-sucking mode. She slap-gifted me with a very charismatic kiss of the tongue sucking extraction nature. Salivating seriously, Jeannie shared with me the sticky taste of sex from kum, sweat, and pussy juice, enhanced and proudly announced the loud flavor provided by champagne bubbles and whipped cream.

About 30 seconds of serving as my little-lady-five-finger, her speed-stroking succeeded. She immediately took her a hand full of come and rubbed it on my chest between my nipples and just above my chicken breast, which I guess she realized had drained out of champagne or been wiped off as she had been performing her body-bootie-scooting act. She quickly filled it again and sprayed more Cool Whip in the shape of an X on my chest. Jeannie then pushed her butt up in the air and used secretions from the split-open-hole between her legs to lubricate and help her ride the slippery slope of my rod so it might let redemption rain down and bring a satisfying comfort to her glorious clitoris. Maybe this is why she referred to it as my little part of heaven.

She leaned forward and slurped all the champagne from my chicken breast. Then motioned to me for a kiss and shared it. She quickly sat straight up on my cock and threw her head back very fast, taking her hair with it.

Her tits had fit perfectly on my chest in the divots where the X crossed without disturbing it. It was absolutely of no significance, just something I had noticed. I thought it was pretty cool that she was so on target she had not messed up my Cool Whip X.

Then she leaned forward a little, flipped her head forward, and her hair came down on my head. As she trailed it down over my face, still staying closely with a swirl connection to my cock, Jeannie gave a couple of little zig-zag moves and she continued her tongue washing and dessert gathering from my come-covered-chest.

Then all of a sudden, she went a little crazy, grabbed one of my ass cheeks in each hand, and held on tight. She began a round-about-ream-out-roll on my rod. Jeannie was really pushing down hard. I was in pretty-deep. I could feel the inner walls of her pussy on the head of my cock. It was limiting the penetration process and applying more pressure with each roll she made on my ramrod in her **red-hot-rotisserie-pussy-lov'n-oven.** Then she gave a moaning groan and started bouncing up and down. Jeannie would ride my cock all the way to the top and slam down hard. She repeated that move over and over and each time she landed she screamed and grunted. Then she started shaking, and the slamming up and down became faster and faster and faster. Jeannie started crying and screaming. She had already put my rocks to bed about five times during this little part of heaven and she was still going strong. Her whole body was motorized. She was shaking like a bucket of paint when they put it on the mixing machine. For about the last 10 times Jeannie slammed down, I was trying to meet her halfway up. Being restrained, I could only push my penis up so far. I could tell it was having an effect by the sexy sounds of her pussy savagely slapping down and swallowing part of my pelvic area while pulverizing my balls. Then I felt her fingernails bite hard into my ass cheeks. Jeannie quickly released my ass-cheeks and began torturing her tits until her nipples achieved hard-on status. They appeared to swell to maybe twice their size. She began to speak so fast the pitch went low then high and totally inaudible.

I knew it had to be soon. The next time Jeannie climbed up my cock-shaft, I lifted my pecker up as hard and as high as the ropes would allow my body to go with my ass. When she slammed down, I held it there. She screamed and flung herself backwards then pulled herself forward and kissed me. My butt was still up off the mat. Jeannie pulled back again and rolled to one side then rolled to the other side. She was using my cock as a reaming ram-rod for her cunt. Jeannie was releasing appreciation moan-groaningly pleasurable sounds of ecstasy for all the rim-rolls and pussy-wall pressure received.

After about two or three minutes of that, Jeannie slid off my cock and rubbed her spread-wide-open-cunt-lips down one leg then up the other one, leaving behind the soft-smooth, warm-wet feeling of love-lava saturated shinbones. She changed her pussy position around so her love nest would land right on my chin. She started caress-kissing my cock and balls in a manner that had only been available to me, at this point in my life, from her super-soft-silky-cock-sucking-lips. This pleasurable performance had always rendered the same response. I muttered in a very low drawn-out tone, "Jeannie-Jeannie-Jeannie." At the same time launching my cock-rocket fast and hard enough to puncture her esophagus and punch a hole in the back of her neck. There I dropped another mother load and choked her half to death. Jeannie hesitated for second of two while she cleared her throat and responded with, "Larry baby, what a good job you did without the use of your hands, thank you very much." Then she began a soft-tongue-traveling-roll around the inside of her mouth process with my pricks-head. Jeannie took my tool on a guided tongue tour of her jaw-bone structure, touching or tapping every part without leaving teeth marks.

We had fallen into my favorite number. Her pussy was so warm and sweet. Remembering the flavor, I said to her, "Jeannie, your pussy is so sweet. How about some champagne saturation?" She obliged and at the same time gave me a little squirt as she spread her pussy lips and squirted more inside. That's all it took and I was engaged in one of the hardest jobs of pussy eating I had ever attempted. I had no way of keeping it tight. If it tried to get away I couldn't stop it. It was impossible to isolate the clit. But it was so warm and sweet and wet and completely edible. I would not have missed it for the world even if I didn't have any control.

I thought maybe this is what she meant when she said hell is just around the corner. It was like craving a porterhouse steak and only being able to touch your tongue to it, or maybe smell it. But it was so good and I wanted to be there so bad that somehow none of that mattered to me. I was going to make it work.

As it turned out I was not the only one determined to make it work. Jeannie was pushing her pussy down on me from just the right angle with force enough I was able to roll her clit with my chin and snorkel snatch secretions with my nose. I was all in. And with that thought, my mind reading Jeannie of the bedroom, mashed her pussy down with more force on my mouth. She was allowing me to enjoy all of that pleasurable warm pussy flavor from the inner lining of her scrumptiousness. At the same time, Jeannie was having a cock-sucking-rodeo. She would switch from time to time from cock-nobbing to ball-blazing. Then she got stuck on sucking my one nut so hard I thought she was going to suck it through its sheath.

For about 20 or 30 minutes, I had been totally dedicated to devouring her luscious love nest. Jeannie was lavishly licking my balls while consciously sucking my cock for the sole purpose of causing the cock to run out of come.

She suddenly decided we would try something different. Jeannie very abruptly brought to a halt a most enjoyable munchie-lunch I was having with her very edible pussy.

For some strange reason, she decided she was just going to squat-touch her pussy to every member of my body that displayed a point of protrusion. First, my nose got a little titillating twat tap. Jeannie then left a trail of love juices across my face and onto my shoulder. She continued her pursuit of never-ending snatch-tapping by straddling my arm with her pussy while setting her sights on my hand. Her cunt seemed to be spreading to a wide-open-faced-pussy-lip-state as she made her way out on my fingers.

Following her pussy travel, I could feel her clit as she spread the lips of her cunt open as wide as she could and force-fed all my fingers into its inner lips. She squatted down a little harder and shaped my four-fingers like a pyramid then started riding up and down on them. I could feel her open-faced pussy's desire to get kinky as she kept pushing down harder with her squats, forcing all four of my fingers deeper inside her split-tail of temptation. It was as though she was trying to engulf my entire hand with her vagina.

Jeannie continued to hold my hand in the upright position while swaying left and right and around and around. The tighter it got, the harder she pushed. Finally, she achieved her goal, Jeannie had spread her love-hole open wide enough and pushed hard enough that her pussy had swallowed my four fingers all the way to the connecting thumb knuckle. The lower valley of her cunt was resting comfortably on the palm of my hand while she directed my thumb into her anal opening. Apparently, this was a sexual maneuver she had become used to and seemed to be enjoying it as she was rocking back and forth.

Jeannie spent the next 5 to 10 minutes finger rocking. She was slipping her pussy up far enough on my fingers to exit, only to begin the reinsertion process while having several-small-tree-trembling-orgasms.

She went to great pains making sure she kept enough pressure on my thumb for anal penetration, then making sure not to show any favoritism. Trembling somewhat, she twat traveled to my other hand and repeated the same process of sexually molesting my limbs of captivity while enjoying repeated small-squalls of sexual secretion.

My prick, however, was a different story. Alone and forsaken, it was standing straight up with a never-ending supply of joy-juice and bountifully bubbling proudly. It had been left lying lonely to sadly saturate the surface surrounding the stump of my shaft with what seemed like an unwanted and wasted supply of my own sexual secretions.

After acquiring orgasmic bliss by force-feeding my fingers deep into her snatch, Jeannie retreated back to slow pussy-surfing of parts unattended. I could feel a sliding-squishy-kinda-squirm as she slid her snatch from nipple to nipple.

My prick was primed and ready to stay, but Jeannie pulled her pussy away; she spread-stretched it down over my knee-cap, squirming somewhat with a squishy sound then a quick release with a snap; and away she goes, headed on down to flavor my toes; from a kneeling position she'd lean back and ride up from little to big, then on to the next foot and start at the top to ride down completing her gig; sucking the extra secretions off of each toe, became the next step, Jeannie did 10 in a row:

********PUSSY POETRY********

xxxxxxxxxxxxxxxxxxxxxxxxxxxxxxxx

pussy poetry is poetry of the soul, expressing one's desires of return to the hole; much like the hole from which you were birthed, your need to return is coming unearthed; to search, to find, those true pussy powers, will control you mentally and physically for hours; once achieved if you should ever do, leaves only one road left for you to choose; you'll spend the rest of your life searching to find, the one pussy that revels you out of your mind:

xxxxxxxxxxxxxxxxxxxxxxxxxxxxxx

When Jeannie had finished with her pussy placing pleasures, I said to her, "Jeannie baby, I understand your desire for dominance and being in control but don't you think I could be a little more helpful if I was not tied down." She looked at me with the look in her eye that told me to forget it.

She never said a word, just turned a little bit, got up, and walked over to the bar and fixed her a drink. Then she looked around and found the drill and the couple other toys that she had there. Again, I said to her, "I know I could be more helpful in every way if I just wasn't being held captive."

Chapter 12
"Return Of The Third One"
"Menage a trios's Forever"

About that time, I heard the door open at the top of the staircase that led to Kristi's room. Jeannie said, "We've had a little change in plans, Larry. I hope you don't mind but Kristi is going to rejoin us for your next episode. She will be bringing your little piece of hell with her."

I thought, well, that's funny, she's not carrying anything and she's not wearing anything. Kristi was casually trailing down the spiral staircase displaying her wonderful womanly wares. She was totally naked. With the first thought that came to mind, I envisioned her lying spread-eagle on a bar. Her luscious delectably delicious looking body had become a muncie-menu for covetously elite lesbian lovelorn ladies. She wore her natural self very well. Kristi had no reason to try to look sexy or sensual. Those characteristics were gifted at birth and she knew it.

I was wondering how she knew when to appear. I did not hear Jeannie call for her and she didn't use the telephone. They must have another way of communicating. Kristi's arrival time must've been preplanned. I am still wondering what kind of hell I'm going to go through.

The next surprise I got was when Jeannie fixed Kristi a drink. From the way she had been talking, I thought she was fixing it for me. But instead, she walked over and met Kristi about halfway from the staircase, handed her a drink, and gave her a kiss. Then she said, "Kristi my dear, have you have been waiting for this with as much anticipation as I have?"

Now I really don't know what the hell is going on. You talk about mixed signals I'm either being lied to or lead on. But they are two beautiful girls so I don't mind too much, except for the fact that I'm tied down.

Jeannie and Kristi walked over to the bar and set their drinks down. They kind of looked at each other and then walked over to what I guess was a storage closet. They pulled out another large workout mat like the one I was laying on, then brought it over and laid it down right beside mine. Jeannie found another sheet that fit the mat perfectly and made it look just like the one I was on.

Kristi went back over to the bar and got the toys that Jeannie had laid out. She brought them over and put them at what would appear to be the head of the bed/mat. Then Jeannie filled up the little roller bar and brought it over to about the same place. They both finished their drink without saying too much.

I was looking around and noticed they had removed some of the mirror fold-outs. I asked if they were going to replace them. They indicated yes, but they would be positioned differently.

Jeannie started to fix another drink so I asked her if I could have one. She told me that she thought it would be best if I stayed sober for this next episode. I did not pursue it any farther.

I had heard about women who got into strange kinky sex-capades. But I had never been involved in one myself. Suddenly, I had the feeling that before this night was over I might be really surprised as to what I would become involved in. I had a lot of questions but I decided to keep them to myself.

They were running around naked, which was very pleasing to my eyes and planted countless want-to's in my mind. Jeannie and Kristi were enjoying their own bare body visuals as well. They seemed to be copping an occasional feel of one another, or a smack on the ass, or maybe even a flip of a nipple. I guess this was their warm-up time before the games began. I suppose it could have been considered lesbian fore-play.

The next few minutes were rather uneventful for me. Jeannie and Kristi were busying themselves having two or three drinks apiece and playing a little touchy-feely with each other's very lovely and willing bodies. They were also making sure everything, including toys and mirrors, were in the right place and properly positioned. I don't know if it's true but it just appeared not to be the first time they had gone through this production.

I was still being ignored or neglected, lying on the mat in a kind of lost and lonely state of lingering limbo mentality, not knowing and trying not to care what was going to happen next. The one thing that was rather disturbing to me was neither one of them were paying any attention to me. That was something I wasn't used to, but I was trying to handle it as best I could.

I was trying to convince myself I was sleepy and maybe I could drop off to sleep. They must have sensed that I was trying to adapt to them leaving me lonely. Suddenly, Jeannie laid a lesbian lip-lock on Kristi that served me up a very large plate of envy. And I can tell you, from that point on, I was filled with nothing but total covetousness. I wanted every fraction of an inch of both their bodies to be within my reach.

The lesbian lip-lock led Jeannie's hand to Kristi's love nest. Suddenly, my dick was hard and I was filled with desires for Jeannie's hand to be wrapped tightly around my shaft. The thought of which brought drool to my tool, but there was very little I could do. I was not only physically bound but I was also mentally bound by lust. I was wishing for more of the pleasures they had both bestowed upon me previously that evening and were now pleasuring each other with.

I'm going to try to stay in touch with you, my literary audience, as much as possible. But I cannot say that I will disclose or portray everything that happened that night in perfect or exact light. But I shall do the best I can while trying to maintain my sanity because after that night I was never the same.

They left me with a very large hole in my heart and just as large of a break in my mind, to say nothing of the most rapid-fire-repeated-hard-on's I ever thought possible. My cock remained red-headed and in a semi-hard or swollen-state for days.

Every time Jeannie or Kristi would invade my space and touch or look at me, my prick would snap to attention and salute them with a constant drool of come. I would be lying if I told you I got over it because I never did. I can tell you one thing for sure: **they put me through a very intentional and extremely seductive lust-filled and coveted adult-rated hell!!!** Now if I may get back to the story at hand.

Jeannie and Kristi were feasting erotically arm in arm. Their hands and mouths were filled with each other's body parts as they made their way to the mat that was right beside mine.

Lamenting, I lay latently my need of their sexual abuse, victimized I am an equal of the color chartreuse; green from envy my blood boiling and my face red, my penis bulging with desire and suffers from being unfed; longing for their touch I harbored a need, that only they could satisfactorily feed; Without one glance in my direction, and no concern for my erection; they put on a show, that would surely blow; the mind that fuses a porno projection; There was no ignoring to be done by me, my vision was impaired and I had to stretch to see; my hands and feet were tied, my mind was warped yet I must abide; while things they were doing for each other they should have been doing for me:

Stopping long enough to fix another drink they strolled casually by. Jeannie made sure to add an extra little sexy bouncing-butt-strut to enhance my hunger, knowing I could tell all they had on their minds was to drive me out of mine.

She walked over to the phonograph and put on a Jerry Lee Lewis record and started rocking out the title. They had obviously practiced this one many times because they had their performance down perfect. Everything was shaken, hair was flying, and tits were boppin'. When they would release from a twirl they'd slide each other's hands over their nipples and create an obvious pinch-pull maneuver. On occasion, when releasing, they let their hands surrender to the magnetic pull of the pussy. They might even try to feed a finger into that split-open-hole between their legs. This, of course, accomplished two things. It started a fire inside of them and fueled the frustrations inside of me.

Then they put on a tape they had obviously created for special workouts. The songs were all songs that could be slow danced to and that is what they did. They were skintight twirl-dipping allowing their pubic hairs to become tangled while tenderly touching twats as they tity-tipped to a tango with their naked bodies.

It is so damned aggravating and demoralizing to be held captive and be forced to watch two very sexy young ladies swapping tongue and finger-fucking each other while dancing nude in front of you.

Very soon, they worked their way around to the side of the mat that was farthest away from me and closer to the tools and drinks. I wondered why they had put things on that side of the mat. When they sat down, they turned around, one on top of the other. Jeannie leaned a little to one side favoring me with a visual snap-shot of their pussy's and asses.

My tongue got immediately hard and pointed. It was probably hanging out of my mouth. My mouth was watering. I had the mix flavored memory taste of both their pussy's on my tongue. That flavor was enhanced by the tangy taste of prune. It was creating quite a loin lament for me that only added to my frustration. And they were just getting started.

They stayed in that position for a short time. I am positive it was to taunt me. Jeannie was on the bottom and she had her legs spread wide apart and bent slightly at the knees, permitting a perfect view of the split-open-hole between her legs, better known to me as the home of **her famous "RED SNAPPER". A miracle worker throughout my dreams of afterglow was oh so sadly soon to be defiled by the infiltration of a strapped on dildo. <u>What a</u> <u>pair of split-tails!</u>**

I have no idea why I chose to punish myself by forcing my head up and stretching my neck out of shape from the tied down horizontal position of my body. Now that's a damn lie and you know it. I was dropping juice like Hollander's goose that got fucked on stage in Amsterdam.

It was actually quite soothing to watch a continuous stream of come shooting out of the top of my cock. It was also fun because my prick was in hard-on status and I could instigate a jerky-ass motion from time to time tossing kum-drops here and there. Unfortunately, I could never toss them far enough to interfere with Jeannie and Kristi's lovemaking.

I learned a lot from watching them take care of each other. They must have truly been in love. When they kissed it was so erotically energetic it gave an appearance of violence. It was almost always as though they were in a devour-ability frame of mind and total consumption was inevitable.

At the beginning, they were especially gentle, and tender, and caring to each other's needs and desires. But once it got started, there was a fire in the hole. Kristi was slapping that pussy like there was no tomorrow. When Kristi thought she was pounding Jeannie's pussy too hard and too fast she would slide off and position Jeannie's body for cunt-licking. That would be the beginning of a gentle mouth massage and pussy eating process. Much to my chagrin, it was being performed by Kristi' mouth and tongue instead of mine.

I found out Kristi knew exactly what she was doing. From her cunt-licking position, she placed her feet on my mat. Using her toes, she managed to scrape around my shaft and the surrounding swap of secretions to secure some of my love juices and take them back to share with Jeannie. The only problem with that was it pissed Jeannie off. She apparently did not want me to have any pleasure, satisfaction, or even slightly enjoy myself. I was obviously tied down to be taunted. **This was my hell!!!**

When Kristi brought herself back into position so that she could share her secretion collection with Jeannie, she got a surprise. Jeannie slapped her and got up immediately. Then said, "You bitch, dammit you knew that is not what this was about." She almost flew up the spiral staircase to her room. I thought her tits were going to bounce off her chest with each step she took. I think she even skipped a step or two.

Jeannie returned with the same speed, urgency, and state of mind that she left with. She was carrying two items in her hands. I didn't recognize one of them but the other one looked like a cucumber or a zucchini. I thought, oh shit, I wonder what she is going to do with that. Then I remembered she mentioned something about vegetables earlier.

It wasn't very long until I found out what the other item was. She hit Kristi on the butt with it and said, "Help me get this damn thing on. I was going to save it for you until later. But you're getting it now Kristi with a K and an I; you are going to get what you deserve. You crossed me, baby, and that is bad."

Jeannie slapped her again, bit one tit and pinched the other one. Kristi yelled and Jeannie pushed her down. She had the double-sided dildo in one hand and grabbed Kristi's hair with the other. Jeannie spread her legs and squatted a little then pulled Kristi's mouth into pussy eating position and said, "Lick my cunt you fucking bitch, get me wet. Lubricate my pussy-hole now because your ass is mine."

I didn't quite understand why Kristi was smiling. Having been treated the way she was being treated, that made no sense. But this whole damn thing didn't make any sense to me. Hell, I'm still wondering what the cucumber is going to be used for.

The licking and lubricating of Jeannie's split-open-hole lasted about five minutes, during which time Jeannie was lubricating one side of the dildo with what appeared to be Vaseline. She would occasionally take a couple of fingers covered with it and present Kristi's prune with several half-assed finger insertions to prepare it for dildo-butt-hole bonding later. Then Jeannie slapped Kristi hard on both ass cheeks only to return to her prune and pussy area to serenade them with several short soft speed-slaps.

Apparently, the proper placing of the double-sided dill-doe's harness and strap buckle was something they needed to work on together. Kristi was kind of squat-sitting on her knees, holding the pecker sections. She held the Vaseline and covered one at the point of entrance to Jeannie's pussy.

Jeannie looked at her and bent down to give her a kiss. It wasn't a long-lasting kiss but it was a tender kiss that said thank you. As she straightened up, Kristi began to push for full artificial prick entry to Jeannie's pussy. Jeannie said okay, then stopped and backed off to a half-open pussy-spread-squat. Kristi immediately took one hand and grabbed Jeannie's ass. Then she began a masterful massage rolling of her ass-cheeks and rectal area. With her other hand, she was creating a teasing ream-rolling entrance for the head of the Vaseline covered dill-doe destined to fill Jeannie's vaginal cavity.

The staff on the dildo was bigger than my cock. Jeannie was having to respond to its entry with a rolling-hip-sway. Kristi was very vigorously continuing her ass-cheek-anal-opening-massage.

The artificial prick was about halfway in Jeannie's pussy when all at the same time she gave a sudden hip-sway. Kristi pinched her ass hard and gave the dildo a sharp push. Jeannie's back bowed out as she screamed and said, "Oh, fuck you, Kristi, that hurt." Then pushed the dildo out and fell on her side holding her tummy. She seemed to be almost crying, or maybe just whimpering a little.

Kristi became very attentive. She began softly rubbing Jeannie's tummy and slowly massaging her pussy area as well as her inner thighs. The two-pronged artificial cock-carrier was abandoned as Kristi proceeded to perform a major mouth-to-pussy surgical massaging process on Jeannie.

In a matter of minutes, Kristi's soft lips had subdued Jeannie's pussy pain to the point that even its memory did not remain. Determined to succeed, they could not refrain. They took the double-sided dick and tried again. **<u>Hoo-ray For Poetic Pussy People!!!</u>**

This time, Jeannie was laying on her back. Kristi was trying to be as gentle and kind as she could after almost causing the blowout of Jeannie's vagina. She tucked a very small pillow under Jeannie's ass. Then she said to her, "Just lay back baby and relax, I will bring you to a very comfortable climax."

Holding the complete package of two cocks and its harness in her hand, Kristi said, "It's better this way and it lines up easier. You should not have been standing the last time. It causes too much strain on the muscles and you must be relaxed. So, my dear Jeannie, as I teasingly touch my tongue to your desirably tender clitoris and perform my own version of mouth to pussy resuscitation, relax and lay back. Dream it is Larry eating your pussy. That thought I know will bring you comfort because he eats your pussy better than anybody else. And rightfully so, you taught him what to do and showed him where to go."

What the fuck is her problem? Here we go again; they're focusing on the irruption of "ole" faithful. They can't be happy if I only have a constant drool. They want to see "ole" faithful blow its top. I mean, here I am lying in a painfully lamenting tied-down-limbo restricted state of body and they won't even jerk me off. All they want to do is talk me off or show me something that causes me to bust a cap. I wish one of them would come over here and sit down on my cock; **I'd bust a double-cap in their ass.**

I could feel the muscles tighten up in the lower part of my shaft and nut sack. I hoped I wasn't getting a cramp. I heard about a guy that got a cramp in his pecker and had to go to the hospital to get a shot for it. Damn, I bet that hurt.

I had been trying not to look while I was feeling sorry for myself when I heard a few little groaning noises and looked over. What I saw was a very sexually arousing sight. Kristi had moved Jeannie onto her side with one leg sticking up in the air and her foot was resting on Kristi's shoulder. She had succeeded in accomplishing full insertion of the vaseline covered cock into Jeannie's prize possession and was strapping on and buckling the harness.

Kristi's ass was sticking some-what up in the air. Jeannie's pussy, plugged with an artificial prick was in full view. The harness had an extra pecker sticking straight out from the one laying claim to Jeannie's vagina.

I guess its first destination will be the split-open-hole between Kristi's legs. After achieving that goal, it would be my guess it becomes time to play the prune-e-e-y tunes. That's a pretty big prick to be sticking up Kristi's ass. I know what happened when she got mine and this one is a hell of a lot larger than mine.

O-O-O-U-C-H!!!

I could tell by the look on Jeannie's face that her vaginal canal was full. Her mouth was stuck at about 1/3 open and she had this oh my "God" look of surprise in her eyes. Jeannie had both hands on her stomach moving them around like she was feeling the dildo changing position as it pressure-pressed the inside of her pussy wall.

Chapter 13
"Pussy Heaven / Hard-on Hell"

Once Kristi had successfully strapped the harness around Jeannie's waist and hips, she took Jeannie's hands and placed them on the un-occupied artificial cock. Kristi then began to very slowly and gently use kind of like a rolling and swaying reaming process to persuade her pussy to open a little wider. That meant, of course, Kristi would have to secure her own mental comfort zone as well.

Kristi gave the artificial cock a soft slow roll and pushed tightly in and around the walls of Jeannie's pussy. Then she began a persuasively sensual, seductively sexy, open-mouthed full-tongue tit-licking trip and upper torso tongue washing. It included a rather lengthy mouthing molestation process on each rib of Jeannie's esophagus. At the same time, she pulled the dildo prick like object out of Jeannie's pussy slightly to ease the pain and help her relax a little. Then gently pushed it back in for full reinsertion of Jeannie's vaginal canal.

Kristi was controlling all of this while her **split-tail-ass-hole-widening ream-job** was being performed by Jeannie. Never losing sight of her objective, Kristi, on occasion, would take one hand and rub her fingers around the widespread lips of Jeannie's cunt. Then she would put them in her mouth, licking them clean of any sexual secretion. She would immediately repeat the fingering-pussy-lip procedure, except this time she inserted her fingers in Jeannie's partially still open mouth while bringing their lips together with tenderness.

This allowed Kristi to provide the easing of Jeannie's pussy pain. It also gave them both a little time-sensitive tongue-tickling. And it would treat them to a few seconds of each other's lips and tongues for a synchronized secretion suck-off.

Kristi so obviously knew what she was doing. After a few minutes of this lesbian-lover-fore-play, Jeannie's mouth was no longer open but **her cunt was open wide.** I very covetously watched her spreading her legs and pussy lips wider and wider to welcome that very large artificial cock that I wanted to trade places with. Instead, I was forced to watch as **it interrupted the magic and ream stretched the walls of her scrumptiousness. Jeannie's Red Snappe**r had been my home away from home earlier in life. **The mental status for my shaft was mostly geared to lust. Now for me to replace this gargantuan cock has become a must:**

********(However)********

The forced entry or raping has bequeathed my mind, with Red-Snapper sadness and sorrow; It leaves me in full concern: will the walls resend with the morrow?

Kristi had lifted her legs up and slid onto the other side of that world of dildos. She had easily accepted its full insertion with a smile. They were sitting somewhat saddle straddling wrapped in each other's arms, while sexually molesting, and lustfully raping each other. They were biting hard and slap-scratching their bodies, tits, and nipples. They were for sure "rockin' that ship."

This must be where Kristi got that term she used on me last night. They were rocking back and forth, and sometimes they would rock halfway up on each other's back, first one way and then the other. Those artificial cocks had to hurt. The more they rocked back, the father the damn thing goes in. It must have been a fucking-foot-long. Yeah, I guess that's where she got the term I recently dubbed a Kristi "Quote": they were for sure **<u>"Fucking The Dog-Shit Outta Each Other."</u>**

The cock-rocking continued and provided several screaming sounds of satisfaction. Screams that profoundly served in the announcing of orgasmic pleasures. While I lay helpless and harmlessly displaying my rod and my staff, they did not comfort me. They just let me lay eagerly overflowing and flooding the soggy bottom part of my ass with what would in time become a wasteland for my love lava.

Oh, but I don't feel sorry for myself. I have been granted the luxury very few men have been afforded. And I can get-off just thinking about it. I had been privileged by being granted the favor of making love to lesbian-lovers. Later, I was given the opportunity to view and critique those same two lesbian lovers performing a complete and absolutely unbelievable tribute to the art of making lesbian love. Which, by the way, there is nothing more wonderfully beautiful than watching two women in total appreciation of the whole of each other's body complete their art of making love. ***<u>I am indeed one lucky son-of-a-bitch!!!</u>*** Aw, but the best is yet to come. I can feel my luck getting better. Soon they will have to get to me. Meanwhile back to the artificial-cock-rockers.

It appeared that Jeannie had become quite fond of that extra-large pecker. I guess she must have loosened up considerably under the instructions and direction of Kristi's expertise. Jeannie seemed to be totally relaxed and moving freely. She was showing no signs of pain with either the reaming or the rocking motion.

I noticed Kristi had started what I thought might be making preparations for a new adventure. It all began with a very solid lesbian love kiss of appreciation that just had to have turned into a tongue-tangler. As she slowly and softly separated her lips from Jeannie's lips with her tongue, she applied a considerable amount of lip-nibbling and chin-nipping. At the same time, she was pulling Jeannie's butt more tightly to the adjoining dildo connection. This reinforced the full insertion by making it ***deeper-and-deeper and more-full of her-prosthetic prick.*** Jeannie's back started to bow-out a little. She made a short grunting sound of relief as Kristi withdrew the force behind her extra-large 12-inch pussy packing prick of prosthesis.

Kristi continued her tongue washing of Jeannie's upper and middle torso, including a hard-sharp tooth, tongue, and lip, suction cup on each tit and nipple. No doubt a celebratory gesture for the pleasures Jeannie had provided her.

Kristi continued the hand squeezing and massaging of Jeannie's ass-cheeks and butt-crack. She masterfully manipulated her mouth maneuvers on Jeannie's titty's, tummy, and bellybutton. As Kristi tongue-twirled Jeannie's bellybutton, she started to slowly pull her butt back. This brought about the releasing control of the artificial cock Jeannie had pushed into her pussy-hole.

When the make-believe prick that had once occupied Kristi's cunt lay in a state of abandonment, both Jeannie and Kristi began to wipe away the love juices with their fingers and feed each other the leftovers.

I guess Kristi decided she wanted to make sure all the pussy secretions were clear. She formed her mouth around the head of the artificial shaft and started an up and down rolling sucking-off adventure, then she attempted to swallow the entire cock-shaft. She soon realized choking would be the reward for not having the talents of deep-throat or a wide enough esophagus.

Kristi then began making preparation for the soon to come introduction of this larger than average oversized prune pleasing prick to her ass-hole. She stuck her fingers into the Vaseline jar and withdrew a good portion. Kristi evenly covered the entire shaft area of the artificial cock and had a little left on her fingers. She reached back and spread her butt-cheeks apart just far enough to properly lubricate the outer edges at the entrance of her prune, then she provided a finger reaming partial insertion. From what I could see, it appeared to be about an inch or inch and a half deep to the inside walls of her ass-hole. The Vaseline would ensure a less painful process for the king-size cock's path of travel to deeper prune penetration.

You could tell she was enjoying this because she had a big smile on her face. She got a little more Vaseline on her fingers and slipped up to give Jeannie a double kiss, one with her lips and one with her lube-job fingers. She announced a premature preview of private prune-popping by a force-feeding application of her Vaseline covered fingers in and around Jeannie's ass-hole.

Jeannie was smiling. Kristi was smiling. They both stood up and Kristi turned her back to Jeannie. Jeannie then reached around under Kristi's arms and grabbed her left tit with her left hand and gave it a momentarily invigoratingly, forceful, and borderline abusive massage. She grabbed a handful of pussy with her right hand and stuck two fingers inside. She put them to her mouth and lips then licked off the juices and said, **"Bend over, baby, and touch your toes, mama's gonna show you where this wild goose goes!!! You know I Love ya, honey, and our love is first-class. I'm going to shove this 12-inch cock right straight up your ass."**

Not one time did either one of them look at me and smile, or blow me a kiss, or say kiss my ass and call me Charlie. I felt like I was as worthless as tits on a boar hog. I wish one of them would have told me to go to hell. At least I could have honestly said, "Open your mouth and I'll go down with a hard-on."

I had a sticking-straight-up-secretion-seeping-shaft that was visibly crying for attention. It may not have been as big but it was begging to compete. I can honestly say it would not have minded playing second-fiddle in this very picturesque process, but I would just have been letting my mouth overload my ass, especially knowing that I was still tied up, or maybe I should say tied down.

Well, so much for good old country clichés. Those old-timers had their shit together. The things they said would fit damn near everywhere.

Hell, man, I've got to get back to the action. It's time for Kristi to get her **prune popped. Well, it's prune pop-poppin' time, yeah it's prune–prune poppin' time; get your prune popped, Kristi, it'll make ya feel fine!**

Kristi had positioned herself kneeling with her body slanting towards the floor from her butt to her shoulders. Her ass was supported by her knees. Her head was resting on her hands that were crossed on the mat they were performing on. Performing is the best word for it because they were putting on quite a show. I would be happy to present them with my **"Oscar, Elmer, or Waldo".** Those were three names given to my cock by three of my mainliners. If we were somewhere and they felt the need to be somewhere else making love they would just say something like, "Honey, don't forget we have to call Oscar later this evening." That was my wife's favorite name for it. The other two would respond in a similar fashion with the other names. I, of course, would take that as a serious signal for their sexual desires and we would get our asses home or find a bedroom somewhere. I have been known to do that.

Jeannie immediately slapped Kristi very hard repeatedly on both ass-cheeks with her hands. Then she reached over and picked up the whip with her right hand. Her left hand was serving as a guide for the extra-large artificial cock. Jeannie was about to infringe upon and add to the pleasures of Kristi's fudge-packing rights.

She had the cock's head resting on the rim of Kristi's ass-hole, ready for entry and primed to puncture her prune. Jeannie slid her hand down over the cock-shaft towards the head and Kristi's anal opening. She was making sure plenty of Vaseline remained on the fullness around the shaft and the prosthesis prick's head.

While her hand was in position, Jeannie decided she would provide Kristi some pre-puncture painless priming pleasures. She slipped her Vaseline covered fingers about two inches deep inside Kristi's butt-hole. Very sensually and slowly, Jeannie began to ream-spread her anal-opening, while whispering sexual sounds for satisfying temptation. She knew this would also secure a soft easy entrance for the big-headed-cock.

With the head of her dildo cock partially inserted and resting in place awaiting the push for penetration, Jeannie forcefully whip-slapped one ass-cheek and then the other several times. It was the offsetting and transferring of the pain process. She was administering the procedure very professionally as though she had done it many times before. Knowing how much Kristi enjoys the back-door-flavor of making love, I would imagine Jeannie got plenty of practice with rear entry.

While the whip-slapping prep was taking place, Jeannie had succeeded in reamingly force-feeding over half of her strapped-on-cock into Kristi's ass-hole. She was continuing her whip-slaps and the slow ream-rolling forward motion acquiring deeper and deeper penetration. Kristi was lending her assistance by providing a perfectly synchronized rhythmic ass-twirling performance.

They seemed to work very well together. To this point, the artificial prick was about two-thirds of full insertion and it didn't seem like Kristi was in any pain at all. That is, of course, with the exception of the whip-slaps that just continued to come.

Speaking of coming, that is precisely what I have been doing constantly, filling up and overflowing the old shaft swap. They should be happy to have created a kum-fountain. If they kept me tied up and keep performing, they could just drop by and get a mouthful of my sexual secretions anytime they desire. Or should they wish to fulfill their need for the flavor of sex, a sentimental moment might be a necessity.

Things were moving along very well, but I just couldn't understand how. I mean that is a BIG-COCK, or large object

Jeannie's forcing up Kristi's ass. It can't go in much farther before Jeannie starts packin' fudge like a bad dog.

****

Then it happened, Kristi let out a scream that could have been heard in Texas and fell to the mat on her stomach. With the falling move, Jeannie managed to keep her make-believe cock connected. She had been able to maintain about 1/3 to ½ insertion but she was laying on Kristi's back and Kristi was crying. Jeannie said to Kristi, "Are you okay, baby? Do you want me to stop?" Kristi replied through her tears and muffled moaning sounds, "No, please, don't stop, please please, don't stop. Just let me lay still for a second."

I could tell Kristi was trying to move her butt for a better position to accept Jeannie's play-pecker. She must have been in pain from the look on her face, but then again, I remember how much she likes this kind of pain.

Working together over the next couple minutes, Kristi and Jeannie returned to their former butt-fucking position. Kristi wasn't crying anymore and Jeannie was not force-feeding that 12-inch horse-cock. Instead, they had returned to their synchronized revolving motions. Jeannie was administering a soft slow rubbing massage to the sides of Kristi's ass-cheeks, back, and hanging down titty's.

Things were getting back to normal with maybe a little more than half insertion of Jeannie's big 12-inch pecker into Kristi's ass-hole. It seemed like Kristi must be feeling better. She had started grinding her ass faster and faster around the shaft of that monster prick that was trying to claim possession of her fudge-factory. She was now doing all the ream-rolling. Jeannie was still standing strong, making sure to keep her want-a-be-cock's partial penetration of Kristi's prune secure. At the same time, she was leaning forward, fondling every loose or hanging part of Kristi's anatomy she could reach.

Jeannie somehow managed to get her hand and fingers covered with Kristi's pussy juices. She transferred the pleasure of sucking and licking them clean to Kristi's tongue, lips, and mouth. Then she played a masturbation melody on Kristi's sexy esophagus.

Wow, I suddenly had a flashback of Kristi's esophagus. That was like an orgasm hanging by a string for me. Just thinking of it generated an automatic nut buster.

Jeannie continued her soft finger roll of Kristi's esophagus and made several trips back to her cunt for reloading with seeping secretions of love lava. One trip Jeannie would make to her mouth for the sucking-off of love-juices, then she would quickly return for more and spread it on Kristi's tummy and titty's while finger-walking back to her tongue and then playing the skin-flute on her esophagus.

Jeannie seemed to really be enjoying the attention she was paying to Kristi's esophagus. I can't say that I blame her, I was enjoying it also, to the tune of what seemed like eternal eruptions while lying there dreaming of the things I'd like to be doing if I were involved in this lovemaking session.

Instead, I'm involved in a love starvation session. But I'm allowed to dream about what I would like to do if I were able to just get free for two or three minutes. They were doing such a fucking fantastic production of prune-popping and double-sided dildo insertion they didn't need my help.

I would just like to honor them for their performance. If I were to suddenly be untied, I would, with cock-in-hand, walk over to them and begin a serenade with a sexual overflow of orgasmic juices that they have built up in my nut-sack, and then continue to spray them with a never-ending masturbation shower of love.

I am sure I could help with bringing them many joy-filled climaxes while watching me become their performance partner from the jerk-off generation. I would keep on keeping on until my come container went dry or my prick fell off.

Kristi must've been watching me or reading my mind. Maybe she had been watching my eyes or something because she was no longer ream-rolling. She was rock-n-roll reaming and begging for more. Then she started screaming: "Fuck me, fuck me, fuck me deeper, push-push-push, jam it deep into my ass-hole deeper-deeper. How much more you got, baby? I want it all, give it to me, give it to me, give it to me now, now-now, even if it hurts, hurt me, hurt me good, hurt me, don't stop fucking me, don't stop fucking me. Jam-it, jam-it, damn-it jam-it in now." Then Jeannie's ass lurched forward and Kristi's back bowed out as she screamed, "Yes-yes-yes, give it to me, give it to me, give me all you got, I want it now, I want it now, don't stop, don't stop, do it deeper, do it deeper, do it deeper-deeper-deeper." Jeannie was holding on tight to the sides of Kristi's ass, and as she gave one violent push, she screamed, "Yeah, here it is, you got it, baby, you got it all!" Jeannie was pounding that prune and doing a drum roll on the top of Kristi's back and buttocks. She gave an occasional pinch or squeeze on a tit and a nipple or just on her sides. Kristi was doing her version of the butt-bounce-boogie with her booty.

You could hear the sexy-sounds-of-slap-slushing-ass-and-pussy-pounding secretions bouncing off the basement walls. The slap-sucking- seductive-sounds of sex's high-volume vibration was making my nuts bounce. It seemed like with every bounce there was another ounce of orgasmic sensation to rock your imagination as to where the hell this was all leading. All the while, Jeannie just kept whip-slapping and slamming that prune. Kristi, though, I don't know how, was accommodating that gigantic 12-inch King-Kong-Cock of gargantuan status. Jeannie had been giving it a guided tour while exploring the depth of Kristi's anal-cavity. Kristi was all smiles; she seemed to be enjoying the intrusive performance of her private-prune-sector.

Aw man, fuck me, I am totally screwed. Now that I think about it, Jeannie's got the opposite side of that artificial-12-inch-play-pecker inside her pussy reaming it out and stretching the walls from hell to Texas. I might as well forget it, even if I fucked 'em all night they wouldn't even know I had been there. Hell, I could never touch bottom, much less provide reaming pleasures to their pussy walls.

I don't have to worry about a damn thing. I'm running so far behind that artificial prick there ain't no way I'd ever be able to catch up. But who knows, maybe they'll give me a chance to try anyway. Maybe they'll let me strap the damn dildo on.

Jeannie and Kristi had been getting it on for quite some time and I knew something had to give pretty soon. I know Kristi has this habit of kind of passing out while she is still connected to her sex partner, what, or whom that may be.

I wasn't sure about Jeannie and how jacked-up that 12-inch-wonder-wand had made her. There was only one thing I could do and that was lay there helpless and wait to see what happened. I just couldn't believe they had both lasted this long. I was getting tired of shooting useless orgasmic blasts just so they could get their rocks off while punishing me.

Then, all of a sudden, it started to happen. I heard moans and groans of ecstasy. I stretched up as far as I could so I could see better and what I saw added to my excitement. I erupted once again, my nut-sack was tight as a drum. I could feel little pains shooting through my container of come. Eventually, it turned its delivery into a constant drool draining down my shaft and onto a swampy-swimming-pool for stuck together hair, which had overflowed and drained off onto the workout mat. It was now a sticky waste-land for my unwanted sexual secretions.

Enough of my sorrows, the excitement is on the other mat with the butt-fuckers and the artificial pussy-packers. The moans and groans of Kristi and Jeannie had inspired hair pulling and the rendering of very hard slaps on the ass and back. Most of the damage was being done by Jeannie. Kristi was still enjoying her rock 'n roll-reaming-my-butt-out-boogie state of mind.

I guess Jeannie was trying to tell us she was having all kinds of dynamic pussy spasms. She was jerking and semi-jumping. Every time she jumped, she drove Kristi a foot closer to the edge of the mat.

Jeannie must have combined three or four orgasmic overloads that took her knees away and she fell forward, landing on Kristi's back. Kristi let out a scream and Jeannie immediately tried to apologize. I guess she didn't have enough energy left to talk so I couldn't understand what she was saying. When Jeannie fell, she rather rudely interrupted Kristi's interior ass-hole massage. Or should I say, Jeannie instigated her own anal anxieties and became the abstracter of Kristi's attempts at pleasuring her perfect little prune.

Jeannie was lying there with one side of that big 12-inch artificial gargantuan pussy and ass-hole plugger sticking out. The other side of it was still submerged deep inside her pussy and held there by a strap.

Kristi looked at Jeannie and said, "You sneaky little cunt, you think you can stop just like that." She immediately rolled Jeannie over on her back, which put her plaything in the perfect position for Kristi's re-mounting and my viewing pleasure. Kristi kind of roll-crawled over to the edge of the mat by the table, grabbed a rather large towel, and crawled back to where Jeannie was lying.

Maybe she couldn't walk, that might be why she crawled. I know if I had that big son-of-a-bitch up my ass as far, and as long as she did, I wouldn't be able to walk.

She grabbed both of Jeannie's legs right at the knees and pulled them tight together. Then she tied the towel as tight as she could around them. Kristi then got into position just over Jeannie's tummy with her knees. She reached over to the Vaseline jar and re-prepped her ass-hole and her most recent favorite toy. Kristi looked at Jeannie and said, "You think you can just take my prick pleasures away? Well, I'll show you, it's my turn now. I am gonna fuck you until I get tired of fucking you. Your pussy will be black, blue, and sore for a month. When I get done with it you'll be begging me to give you pussy massage with Aloe Vera oil. Maybe I can saturate a Kotex with it and you could use it for a dildo."

Jeannie was just lying there laughing but she wasn't laughing long. Kristi started sliding her recently lubricated make-believe gentlemen's joy-stick along her butt-crack and into position for entry of her ass-hole. Kristi must've been red-hot and primed. It only took about a minute and she was pumping Jeannie's pussy with all the pressure she could bring from her pruning partner. The very first slide-stroke produced a pain-filled sound from Jeannie's lips.

Kristi had chosen a position so she could roll forward and catch herself with her knees on either side of Jeannie's ass-cheeks, or she could roll back a little and let her butt rest on Jeannie's upper thighs. And this meant either way she rolled, it would be putting pressure for deeper penetration on the already inserted buckled up dildo that was meant to be pleasure searching Jeannie's vaginal canal.

Kristi was bound and determined to raise some sort of verbal response from Jeannie, which so far had not surfaced. She slowly started to be more sensual by leaning forward a little so she could start nipple-pinching and tit-rolling. Kristi brought Jeannie's hand back with her and helped her force-feed a couple of fingers deep into her unoccupied, but always ready for action, pussy. Together they accomplished a most favorable job of duet-finger-fucking. It was also very turn-on-ish to watch the rhythm of Kristi's body match the rhythm of Jeannie's fingers for deeper pussy penetration.

Kristi then lifted herself on her knees and moved forward a little farther so that she could transfer some of her pussy juices to Jeannie's mouth. This did Kristi's rear entry partner the favor of deeper delivery into her ass-hole. At the same time, it produced a mouth opening gasp for breath from Jeannie that brought a devilish smile to Kristi's face. She had intentionally moved forward, causing extra pressure to be applied to the big-12-inch-pussy-packer that Kristi now seemed to be using as a crutch to help hold her body up.

The next thing Kristi did was absolutely ridiculous. It could have and probably did hurt her very much. She sat straight up on that 12-inch-mother-fucker, then she surrendered control of her ass-hole by moving her feet from the floor to Jeannie's shoulders. This forced all her body weight to be resting on that big-Vaseline-greased-lightning-hand- made carpenters-cock.

In one second, with a sudden jolt, Gargantuan traveled to its totality. It favored Kristi with the fullness of her ass-hole. She never made a sound. She threw her arms straight out, grabbed Jeannie's tit's and pinched them hard, then returned to reinforce the grip she had on her own tit's and pinched them even harder. She was applying a self-tit massage that screamed of violence with the portrayal of harmful intent. Kristi then threw both hands straight up in the air grabbed her hair and started to jerk and pull.

I had no idea what she was doing at the time. However, as years went by, I learned that pain of the heart, mind, body, or soul, I suppose, can be offset or compensated for by creating or inducing a greater pain to a comparable body part. Kristi had mastered the art of compensating for pain. Her mouth was open. And once again Jeannie began to jerk-off her esophagus. She individually, very gently finger-rolled each rib of Kristi's sensationally sexy enticingly invitational throat that was demanding attention for esophagus travel.

If only I were not tied down, maybe I could master the art of compensating for the pain her sexually enticing esophagus is subjecting me to. I could jack-off all over her voluptuousness, bringing my journey to an end being pleasured by traveling her tubular tunnel of esophagus love with my rock-solid shaft. **"Damn, am I dreaming again; that's a pretty good dream I love to dream."**

It seemed like now that Kristi ass-hole was once again enjoying the sensation of being fully plugged by that 12-inch phony prick she couldn't be hurt anymore. She had returned to her back-door rock-a-bye-butt-hole-baby moves. Now she was determined to produce more penetrating pleasure or pain for Jeannie's spread-wider than wide and solidly packed-split-open-pussy-hole.

And so the screams began as she pushed forward with her positraction ass and was holding on tight to Jeannie's ass-cheek-bones to prevent her from sliding back and lessen the pain. Jeannie immediately saw what was happening and screamed out, "No, Kristi, no, please don't, please do not do this. I will do anything you say and you can do anything you want but please don't do this. You know it hurts me so much, please don't." Kristi replied, "That all sounds really nice but I also know how much you like it." Kristi had purposely used forceful and very abrupt prosthetic-cock-slamming moves. She was preparing mentally for self-satisfaction from the punishment she was putting Jeannie's pussy-walls through. Kristi had to be causing lots of pain to herself with that fabulous-foreign-object-up-her-ass. Still, she kept pounding forward into Jeannie's love hole, driving her big 12-inch cunt-filler deeper and deeper and forcing her vaginal tunnel of love to extend its boundaries.

Chapter 14
"Revenge of The Prosthetic Prick"

Jeannie's screams and crying became louder and the pain of penetration more obvious, then suddenly they stopped. Not one tear was in Jeannie's eyes. Instead, the look of intense anger filled her eyes and her entire face tightened. She reached up and grabbed both hands full of Kristi's hair. Jeannie used it for leverage to pull herself up and began bouncing up and down, around, back and forth, then she cried out, "You good for nothing cunt-licking artificial cock-sucking lesbian bitch. I told you never, ever do that again under any circumstances. Now you better give your heart to "God" because your ass belongs to me you back-door loving bitch. I'm gonna tear you a brand-new ass-hole with this big rubber gargantuan piece of shit substitute for someone who can't get a real cock large enough to satisfy her anal anxieties."

Jeannie kept one handful of hair and the other one on Kristi's shoulder. She began a fast sharp rocking process with her ass moving in every direction and a look of pain-filled-anger on her face. She released an angry grunting sigh with every move she made. Her back was beginning to bow out, obviously caused by the pussy-pains she was experiencing.

I wasn't sure if Jeannie was mad or she was just getting into the feeling of what was going on. All I really knew was my neck was beginning to cramp and get stiff. I had to lay my head down to rest every now and then.

I had been watching this lesbian liaison for I guess an hour, maybe longer. I raised my head back up to rejoin the action, only to find the tables had been completely turned. Kristi was back on her knees and Jeannie was pumping her from behind. She had also added the attraction of anger, forcing all of her fingers into Kristi's cunt and working them in a violently vigorous pussy pounding process. Kristi's head was resting on her hands. Jeannie was pile-driving the artificial cock farther and farther into her ass-hole while she was sucking-off the love juices on her fingers and hand that she had stolen from Kristi's cunt.

Jeannie had got to the point where she seemed to enjoy the painful process she was putting Kristi through. But I know from first-hand experience you really don't know if Kristi is enjoying the pain too much or what she's doing for sure. The only way you find out is when she passes out from the pain; then you know she is enjoying the pain too much to stop and will soon be ready to go another round.

They both seem to be in very good shape physically to have survived this continuing competition for as long as they have. Although Jeannie had regained the role of dominance, Kristi wasn't really complaining. Instead, quite the opposite seemed to be occurring. It was like she was enjoying the butt-hole-bonding that prosthetic cock created while being viciously jabbed in and out to secure deeper penetration of her anal cavity.

Using Kristi's hair for somewhat of a leverage bridal, Jeannie began the rolling-bump of horseback riding rhythm. She was slapping Kristi hard with the **whip** from side to side. Each punishing-pump of the prosthetic-prick-provided Jeannie more pile-driving pleasure and Kristi more pleasurable pain. With every rodeo rhythm bounce and whip-slap, Kristi gave a pain-filled scream and begged for more. And that's exactly what she got.

Jeannie's face was filled with fire and fury. Her pain-filled anger was translated by words of demons in the voice of the devil. She began to bellow, "So you want more, you fucking back-door-whore. Well, maybe you'll like this." She incorporated in her ride the bounce of a bucking bronco. So much so her knees crashed down hard to the floor on several occasions. Each bounce was accompanied by a whip-slap on either side of Kristi's hips and ass-cheeks. Jeannie was also producing a seriously painful push-shove-jab-jamming process on the artificial-cock that must have already traveled through Kristi's throat on its way to her mouth.

I was expecting its head to pop through her lips at any time. I could almost see it tipping over each rib of her esophagus while fucking it on the way up. That thought alone brought pleasure to my prick as it pleasingly produced another prize pain through my nut-sack.

Kristi was crying and screaming and Jeannie must've been creaming. She was shaking and quivering with her mouth wide open. She had to be coming but it wasn't going to stop her from pounding King Kong's Prong farther into Kristi's ass-hole. It seemed like she had only one thing on her mind and that was to cause Kristi as much pain as she possibly could. The feeling of conquering Kristi was cover for her own pain.

She continued with her ass-slapping prick-pounding rage by pulling back on Kristi's hair to gain leverage and provide more power for pecker pounding. I almost felt sorry for Kristi, she had to be losing some hair.

Jeannie was right in the middle of delivering a slamming ramrod to Kristi's butt-hole when, just as the cramming contact was made, Kristi fell flat on the mat. The snapping crack-back-shock of the sudden-stop must have done one hell of a jam-job on Jeannie's-twat. She had the power of the ramming force plus her weight slamming down and was brought to a very abrupt halt on the artificial cock that occupied her cunt. She went crazy screaming and crying, pulling Kristi's hair hard and falling backwards. Jeannie unbuckled the harness, and with tears falling freely, she gently pulled the phony-prick out of her pussy. Then she let go of Kristi's hair and quickly yanked the fully inserted artificial-gigantic-rodeo-cock out of her ass-hole. Upon its exit, we were serenaded with a series of slapping-pops and bubbling-farts, but no response from Kristi. She was still lying motionless on the mat. Jeannie screamed out, "You butt-fucking bitch, you better wake up. I'm going to show you what it's like!"

Jeannie got to her feet as quickly as she could but was partially bent over with pain and moving slow. She picked up the prosthetic pricks and gingerly made her way to the bathroom. I guess that's when she washed and sanitized the double-sided dildo.

I knew there was nothing I could do to help Kristi so I just laid my head down to rest my neck and waited for Jeannie's return. In a couple of minutes, she returned to the mat and was busying herself re-lubricating only one prick on the double-sided dildo. She still had that look of anger-pain on her face. She went over to the bar, poured them both a drink and left them at the bar.

I sure as hell didn't know what to expect next but I didn't expect what happened and I'm sure Kristi wasn't expecting it either. When Jeannie got back to the mat, she repositioned Kristi by turning her over on her back and pulling her closer to the middle of the mat. Kristi was still not responding.

Jeannie never said a word to Kristi; she just spread her legs as wide apart as she could until her pussy was positioned perfectly for my limited line of sight. I could see everything that was going on. I think Jeannie did that as a favor to me. I guess she thought I needed a few more nuts busted; thank you, Jeannie.

Kristi was still lying flat on her back and motionless. That's when I realized what was about to take place. Jeannie put Vaseline on both hands, and with pissed off roughness used one hand to apply it to Kristi's pussy lips. The application was administered by three or four rather hard pussy-slaps. Hell, knowing Kristi's love for the pain, she probably had an unconscious orgasm. With the other hand, Jeannie began to lubricate her pussy. The scenery was not only lustfully beautiful but very sexy as well. I could feel myself creaming again.

Jeannie got up, walked over to the bar, and got her drink. Then she turned and said to Kristi, "Would you like a drink, Kristi? I'm about to do the boogie-woogie on your pussy walls. Maybe that will wake you up. I know for sure it will let you know how I felt."

Five minutes must've gone by and there was still no movement from Kristi. I wasn't sure if she was passed out, playing possum, or dead. I remember her passing out episodes lasted a long time during my trips of anal intrusion. I personally felt that she was probably playing possum. She might've been listening to everything that Jeannie was saying and just preparing herself mentally to accept whatever came her way.

Jeannie was in a sort of sit-leaning position beside Kristi and behind one of her spread-eagle legs. She took the pretense prosthetic prick in her right hand, holding Kristi's cunt-lips open with the thumb and forefinger of her left hand. Jeannie leaned forward a little and I thought for a second she had a pussy eating urge. But I was wrong, she just leaned over and gave Kristi's clit a couple tongue slaps.

Kristi and Jeannie were really something else. They knew exactly where to go and how to do what needed to be done without having to search for a pathway to procure the process. They both appeared to favor a little badmouthing and name-calling during sex when possible. It seemed to enhance their mood or maybe even serve as a turn on.

Once Jeannie had licked Kristi's clit it was like she had been cleared for cunt clobbering. She placed the point of the make-believe monster cock inside the spread open mouth of Kristi's pussy. When the want-a-be prick's head was securely wrapped with Kristi's cunt-lips, Jeannie took her left hand and grabbed her by the hair again. Then with almost the same rhythmic motion of her body, she began pushing and ream-rolling the artificial cock into Kristi's love hole.

There was still no movement from Kristi. I guess Jeannie decided to shock her back to consciousness. She gave the stub of the dildo what amounted to probably a 2-inch jamming jab inward. Kristi immediately tried to set up and her eyes popped open. She was gasping for breath as she very quickly sucked her stomach in. Jeannie yelled out, "You possum playing bitch." And immediately pulled hard on her hair to get her back down and then straddled her. She was sitting with her ass right on Kristi's tits while maintaining the inserted position of the playgirl-cock.

I felt myself cringing at the thought of it and feeling sorry for Kristi. That damn thing was as big around as a good size cucumber. That would be about twice as big around as mine and she was hurting when she took it. I don't want to compare the length, I know I'm way too short for that.

Needless to say, Jeannie was certainly able to get Kristi's attention. There can no longer be any doubt about her present state of consciousness. Kristi didn't seem to be providing much resistance if any. This led me to believe that she probably enjoyed looking straight into or around Jeannie's butt-crack and asshole. That would keep her true and in possible hot pursuit of her lovemaking lustful lure.

While Jeannie was flattening Kristi's breasts, she was still performing the artificial-cock-ream-roll and plastering Kristi's pussy with pain. She still held dominance from the handful of hair. She was pulling it hard enough over her shoulder to lift Kristi's head to the point where her nose could not be any more than a couple of inches from the entrance of her ass-hole. Knowing Kristi's favorite place to go made the method to Jeannie's madness obvious.

With Kristi's hair stretched tightly over her shoulder, Jeannie began to give an unbelievably sexy performance. After attaining a semi-squat position, she was barely touching Kristi's titty with her but-cheeks. Kristi's face was almost buried in Jeannie's ass-crack. Jeannie then administered to Kristi's boobs a soft-swirling-buttocks-squat-massage. This, because of the controlling hank of hair, made it impossible for Kristi not to become involved. Kristi's face was keeping pace with that soft swirling move of Jeannie's ass as it gently swayed from side to side over Kristi's tender tits, providing them with such sensation it afforded me the luxury of watching her nipples swelling to hardness.

The handful of hair was released and Jeannie repositioned her lesbian-love-nest perfectly for Kristi's partaking. Her ass-hole and lower pussy area lay in total submission to Kristi's tongue.

Their bodies began to sway in unison. Jeannie's tits took a tantalizingly titillating tour of Kristi's tummy as she tongue traced the upper edges of her twat. Jeannie started working her ass with a sexy invitation to the sensually soft sweetness that flowed in sync with Kristi's lips and tongue.

She continued to apply the pressure on Kristi's pussy-walls by force-feeding what now has become both of their favorite playthings. The prosthetic-prick was finding its way deeper and deeper into Kristi's-cunt and stretching her vaginal parlor.

It didn't seem like Jeannie was hurting Kristi at all. What it really seemed like was that every time

Jeannie would go deeper into Kristi's vaginal parlor, Kristi would begin a more intensified and interestingly vigorous ass-licking and clit-clinging performance on Jeannie's pleasure **holes.** She would on occasion, after accepting the pussy-pain presented to her by the prosthetic-prick, violently smack Jeannie on the ass, sometimes even leaving a handprint. Otherwise, Kristi's hands were usually occupied by assisting Jeannie with the magical moves of her ass to better determine its tightness to her tongue.

To this point, Jeannie had succeeded in accomplishing about two-thirds insertion of the artificial cock into Kristi's pussy. It appeared that the pissed off ugliness and anger pains had evolved into a very compatible lust-filled lesbian lovemaking session, one I was finding very entertaining and orgasmically satisfying.

When Kristi's hands were not busy motivating Jeannie's ass, she would be trying to replace the joy-stick by finger-fucking her with one hand and titty-tossing with the other. I could tell, and I'm sure Kristi could tell as well, Jeannie had been gifted with several clitoral tremors. She was quivering and shaking to the point of almost neglecting to deliver the long overdue and promised pay-back pussy-pains to Kristi's cunt.

Then like she had read my mind so many times before, she began a high-speed masturbation maneuver on Kristi's-pussy with the prosthetic- prick. Jeannie was no longer trying to force-feed the gigantic replica of a horse's cock. Instead, she was using it with her hand in a manner that resembled the rapid-fire in and out motion of the normal pussy-fucking process.

Kristi was experiencing a continuous come with tsunami-like turbulence and was showing her appreciation to Jeannie with a merciless performance of mouth to pussy presence. She was going after that vagina flower as though she was starving to death and hadn't eaten in years.

Then I heard Jeannie scream out, "Here it is, you got it now!" It looked like she had doubled her moves of masturbation on Kristi's pussy. The artificial cock had completely disappeared and Jeannie was performing her victory celebration at Kristi's cunt. Kristi was bouncing around like she was trying to get into Jeannie's pussy head first. They were both slap-happy and pinching each other. They were so hot for each other their boilers blew and generated a heatwave of dual proportion as they collapsed together with quivering climaxes.

I heard Jeannie saying in an almost out of breath and gasping voice, "I got ya, baby, you took that whole damn thing." Suffering from the same out of breath manner, Kristi came back with, "I know, and oh, you made it feel so good. Jeannie, you are so good to me and so good for me. I love you so much. And you make it hurt so good." I thought to myself, *damn what a familiar line.* I wonder if she tells everybody that.

Totally spent, they laid there together in each other's arms and didn't even bother removing the prosthetic prick from Kristi's pussy. They were almost perfectly still for about five minutes. That gave my neck a well-needed rest.

I heard them starting to move around so I lifted my head to see what was going on. They were just playing little touchy-feely love games. Together they removed the larger-than-life masterpiece from Kristi's tunnel of love.

Finally, they both looked over at me and smiled. Then Kristi asked me, "How are you doing, Larry?" I replied, "I'm doing just fine, other than being saturated with 5 gallons of unwanted love juices. I enjoyed it. Y'all are very good teachers. I have learned a lot and I'm ready to go. It is my turn now, isn't it?"

Chapter 15
"It's My Turn"

I didn't get a response and they just laid back down together. I watched them play their little touchy-feely, kiss a nipple, bite a lip, hump the thigh moves for a minute or two. Then I laid my head down to rest my neck. I figured they'd untie me when they got ready. I didn't have any reason to complain. I had been enjoying a very enlightening and extremely entertaining getting reacquainted party with Jeannie, along with so many extra satisfying pleasures of love bestowed upon me by Kristi.

I must've dozed off for a second or been dreaming because the next thing I remember was when Jeannie straddled my lower torso and sat down on my cock. She had brought what was left of the bottle of Dom Perignon with her. She poured the glass about half full while she was rotating her pussy around in a circle on my prick. I couldn't have been sleeping because I still had a hard-on, although, it didn't do any good. I couldn't feel the walls or the bottom of her stretched out of shape bottomless pussy-pit. Even with her performing her little sexy circle of molestation on my shaft, I could barely tell I was there. It looked very nice but I knew damn well it wasn't doing anything for her.

Jeannie leaned forward until her tits were almost in my mouth and I still couldn't feel the walls of her pussy rubbing against cock. She offered me a drink and I raised my head. As she tipped the glass toward my lips, she said, "Larry baby, you have been such a good sport about all this so I'm going to tell you that the best is yet to come. Of course, you may not consider it the best. It just might be the worst for you. Your love-stick hopefully has not been overcharged from the pleasurable performances Kristi and I have provided for you this evening. I will have to say it has created a very slippery saddle for me to straddle. Hell, I couldn't sit still if I tried. I guess it all depends on how much you have left in your tank of talents to give."

She helped me take another drink and then gave me a little kiss as she turned herself into a merry-go-round, using my cock as the wobbling center support rod. I asked her again, "Jeannie, do you intend to keep me in bondage forever?" She replied, "Relax, Larry, it'll be okay. Besides, I've had a little change of heart. Since you were so good to Kristi and Kristi was so good to me, we've decided it is our turn to return the favor. However, I guess good can be defined by how well we all perform. Don't you just love surprises like this?" I replied, "To be very honest with you, I've never had a surprise like this. Oh, by the way, what time is it?" She responded, "Don't worry you'll have plenty of time to get to work after we are finished. But if you don't and you should get fired, Kristi and I will make sure you have a job. We're finally back in touch after all these years and you don't really think I will let you get away again, do you?"

She stood up and as the warmth of her pussy abandoned my cock, there were no sexy slushing sounds or pops of pussy farts. There was so much excess air in her vagina canal surrounding my prick I couldn't feel any difference when she slid off. Jeannie then said to me, "Larry, you should lay back and rest a few minutes. We're going to go upstairs and freshen up a little.

When we return, you will be the recipient of what most men could only dream of." I laid my head back and shut my eyes. I think I actually fell into a never-ending dreamy wonderland of afterglow. I was frolicking in the warmth of Jeannie's Red Snapper during my training exercises.

New Chapter 16
"My Body Washing Serenade"

The next thing I remember, they were standing naked at my sides looking down at me. They had restyled their hair. Jeannie had a ponytail and Kristi had rolled hers up in a perfect little bun on top of her head. They looked scrumptious and wore mother-nature very well.

(A very nice dream to wakeup to!!!!! Or in)

They were armed with a basting brush, a new bottle of Dom Perignon, champagne glasses, bendable straws, and a can of Cool Whip. On their faces were devilish smiles of sin and sex as they traced their tongues back and forth while cunningly suck-caressing the protrusion points of each other's upper lips.

They both set what they were carrying down on the stand, and as they turned around, they pleasured each other with a loving lip-lock. Then together began a body fondling lip-molesting trip. They traveled from mouth to neck to tits to twats. Kristi dropped to her knees and her tongue went immediately to Jeannie's love-nest in search of her glorious clitoris. Jeannie spread her legs enough for Kristi to lay down on her back and slide her body between them.

Kristi was now providing a perfect view of Jeannie's scrumptiously edible, deliriously delicious pussy parts and anal orifice, which she coveted every minute of every day. It sure as hell looked good to me. If Jeannie's pussy had been stretched out of shape, there were no visible tell-tale signs of monster cock molestation. I felt certain it would return to its normal size soon enough.

Jeannie then bowed her knees with perfect muscle control and lowered her body as she placed her pussy on Kristi's anxiously awaiting mouth. What a perfect picture. **Jeannie was sitting flat on Kristi's face.** I watched and drooled as Kristi's tongue partook of the sweetest, most edible fruits of her lesbian lover. What a turn-on—I just kept flooding the swamp with my come.

Jeannie saw what was happening with my wantonized-cock. She knew she was close enough to me that if she stretched a little she could grab my cock and gather some love juice to take back and share with Kristi. And she did just that. During Jeannie's pleasuring process, she smiled and mimicked me a kiss. Then favored my prick with one sliding up and down jerk-off move and my cock runneth over.

She took her hand, covered it with want-to-be Jeannie's jack-off-juice, and placed it between her cunt and Kristi's lips. Then Jeannie began to rock-n-roll her pussy on Kristi's face. Jeannie put both hands close the back of Kristi's head and pulled her mouth tighter to her pussy and they both went nuts. Their bodies were constantly moving one way or another. At one point, Kristi's legs were sticking straight up in the air and shaking while she was lavishly lip-sucking and taste-testing Jeannie's lesbian love hole. Jeannie was responding to Kristi with the most energetically invigorating charged face-fuck she could muster. Both verbally and physically, she brought thunder sounding smacks of pussy pounding pleasure to Kristi's hungry mouth. The pussy pleasuring constituted a colliding connection so furiously fast and forceful it created a cloudburst of Jeannie's come. Jeannie had treated Kristi to a full-course meal of delirium through the guise of her treasured-taste-test of lesbian-love-lava. This began the feasting process.

It was so exciting I couldn't take my eyes off them. Through the help of the mirrors, I was able to rest my neck a little and still watch their fantabulous performances. They displayed unbelievable desires for the devouring of each other's personal prize possessions. Jeannie had turned a full circle and still remained in a perfect position for Kristi's pussy pleasuring. That masterful move put her mouth in position to provide Kristi's pussy a reciprocal pleasuring process. She made her mouth to Kristi's pussy connection with one loud slobbering sound of suction as she clamped her lips tightly around her clit and provided Kristi with a couple minutes of thunderous tornado-like pleasurable pussy pain.

It was very easy to tell that Jeannie was the dominant force of this performance. She exhibited a perfect example for Kristi to follow the leader with no resistance. Jeannie broke her mouth connection to Kristi's pussy and started slip-sliding her body backwards up to Kristi's head. That had also caused Kristi to break contact with Jeannie's cunt. They both performed a mouth-body surfing and kiss caressing process on each other that left nothing for the imagination. I became privy to the sights and sounds of nipple nursing, bellybutton and body sucking, armpit licking, and the final coming together of an upside-down lovingly long and lingering lesbian lip-lock. Then they retraced their steps. And as they reached mouth to pussy resting places became engaged in what turned into a wonderfully beautiful display of pay-back pussy eating. They shared what seemed like had become a never-ending fulfillment of Jeannie's earlier physical agreement for each other's pleasuring.

I was having major nut pains from being forced to generate many-many orgasms only to be released as a constant drool of my tool. Something was keeping me from erupting normally. There were no more explosions or shooting straight up in the air, just a drooling tool.

All of a sudden, I got hit in the back of the head with a memory from a couple of years prior. An old roommate of mine came home late one night after the date. He was walking all straddle legged. When he closed the door behind him, he dropped his pants and underwear, then grabbed his cock and balls and almost crawled through the room. I said, "What the hell's wrong, man?" He painfully grunted, "That fucking bitch took me all the way to the point of no return and wouldn't even suck me off. Man, I got a bad case of blue balls." Oh well, so much for my-lovers-cramp pains; at least I didn't get them the way he got his.

Let's get back to the pleasures, maybe it will produce more pleasurable pain this time around. Maybe they will untie me.

I had shut my eyes for a second or two. When I opened them, I was watching Kristi initiate a very interesting and almost savagely violent change of position. She had stuck the thumb of her right hand into Jeannie's ass-hole and managed to grab her ponytail with the other one. Kristi was physically overpowering Jeannie and forcing her down to the mat, using Jeannie's ponytail to pull her down and her prune puncturing thumb to push and apply more painfully enticing pressure. Kristi succeeded in the role reversal and acquired the dominance of being topside.

Her interest now seemed to be getting Jeannie in position to eat her pussy while lying flat on her back, just the way she had been. In other words, a complete body position change. The easiest way would just be to say "alright, role reversal, or it's my turn to be boss." But that would not provide the pain or excitement and bragging rights.

Jeannie was resisting by trying to out muscle her. But that was not going to happen. Kristi gave a yank on the ponytail and a hard push on the prune-finger. Jeannie scream-grunted and quickly assumed the bottom position and began to administer Kristi's clitoral satisfaction.

Kristi brought her house down. She remained in possession of her ponytail and prune lodging. Jeannie had no choice except to render Kristi helpless through the means of her mind-blowingly masterful miracle-working mouth to pussy massage.

Jeannie knew were to go, what to do to which part, how to nip-bite, and when to tongue travel. It wasn't long until Kristi let go of the ponytail and removed the thumb. She brought both hands to either side of Jeannie's face and started crying and professing her love for Jeannie's talented tongue. Soon they were arm in arm rolling around on the mat, kiss-molesting and diget-fucking every bodily orifice within reach. They had both been sexually subdued by Kristi's innovative ways of providing Jeannie with a lesbian-love-hole-lunch and lay satisfyingly motionless for a few moments. And so was I!!!

Chapter 17
"Champagne Cock-Tails"

After a short recovery period, I heard them moving and talking about the evening's actions of satisfaction. Kristi had taken a drink of champagne but did not swallow it. She slipped her lips over the head of my prick then opened her mouth, letting the bubbles treat my entire cock-shaft and nut-sack to a pleasurable champagne cooling saturation.

They both sat down on the mat, either leaning on one hip or Indian style on each side of me. Jeannie leaned over, putting her lips around the head of my cock while using her tongue to ride the rim. Then she applied full strength esophagus-suction and pulled her mouth off the head of my prick really fast, which produced the sexy sound of a slapping-pop. Kristi immediately placed a dab of Cool Whip perfectly covering the eye of my cock and spray-wrapped a ring around the head. Jeannie had her hand tightly wrapped around the base of my shaft near my nut sack and began working a semi-jerk-off move from that area. She made sure to keep a tight grip on my cock as she worked her way up to the head. Her hand and my foreskin formed a perfect cock-skin cup. Kristi had taken another drink of champagne but not swallowed all of it. She slipped her lips down over the head of my prick again, this time coming to rest on Jeannie's hands. Jeannie proceeded to have a taste of champagne-cock-tail with cool whip. Then she began her high-powered vacuum suction and swallowed some of the cool whips. She started pounding my pecker with repeated precision until I busted a nut in Kristi's mouth. The evening's appetizers were Dom-perignon-cool-whip and come-drops. As Kristi suckingly stripped the head of my cock and treated it to a tongue-lapping-massage, she glanced over at Jeannie with a look of invitation to share. Kristi then pulled her lips together over the head of my pecker with the slurping sound to save the secretions of sex. Jeannie quickly took the head of my prick in her mouth to claim anything left over. And then they kissed. I could see their mouths, their jaws, their lips, and their tongues moving the excess mixture around from side to side. At the same time, Kristi's hand had found my cock and they were milking me with rhythm. Suddenly, the sexy sounds of esophagus-suction produced a double slurping-slap from the duet's satisfaction of swallowing, while the outlet of the "ole" jizzum-trail, once again, began to bubble over with pride of a continuous drooling fashion.

These gals were truly honest-to-goodness **SPLIT-TAILS!!!** Deserving of---**SPILT-TALES!!!**

Chapter 18
"Body-Part-Dessert"

I couldn't wait to find out what was next. As it turned out, I didn't have to wait long at all. Once they had equally shared the evenings hors d'oeuvres, they began diligently working at preparing the main course, which appeared to be leaning toward a massive dessert. Kristi was in charge of the cool whip and Jeannie the basting brush. I had no idea what she was going to use it for.

Jeannie walked over to the table where they had set the champagne along with other items and picked up a jar of strawberry jam. She stuck the basting brush in the jar of strawberry jam and twirled it a couple of times to make sure the brush was well saturated. Then she took it immediately to my nut sack at the base of my main vein and glazed my entire shaft with strawberry jam. Jeannie dabbed a light glazing on her pussy lips and kneeled down to present a teasing taste for my outstretched tongue, which had been patiently awaiting the sweetness of her strawberry snatch.

While I was pleasing the both of us by pleasuring Jeannie's pussy, Kristi had coated my cock with Cool Whip and was successfully swallowing my strawberry glazed ram-rod with Cool Whip topping.

Jeannie suddenly realized she had a lot of prep work to do before Kristi could put on the final touches. She kind of slow-crawled straddling my nose and forehead with her strawberry flavored pussy. Jeannie favored my arm by allowing her cunt to spread a lightly flavored glazing on it as her pussy-lips opened for the split-tail-trip to my fingertips. She carefully glazed each digit then moved to the other hand and did the same. Then she reversed the procedure of flavor-filled traveling titillation for my other arm and back to my tongue. I continued to strip her pussy lips of all strawberry flavoring. She dipped her basting brush a couple more times and glazed a trail of continuous zig-zags on both arms from my hands back to my neck, including my armpits. In the meantime, Kristi had completely suck-stripped my nut-sack, shaft, and cocks head of all its sticky sweeteners. The only thing about Kristi that remained sticky was her lips. I noticed when she was on her way to my hands to apply her portion of prep work she hesitated long enough to favor me with a taste of her tongue.

It seems the idea was, everywhere Jeanie had brushed a glazing of strawberry jam, Kristi would apply a topping of Cool Whip. Jeannie was now working on my chest, circling my nipples and lightly glazing the tit-nipples. As it turned out, she would go from there to my bellybutton then all of my lower torso and crotch area, including my ass-hole. Jeannie totally traveled my legs. She treated them to torturingly treasured touches that inspired pleasure to her tantalizingly teasing twat of Red-Snapper temptation while tipping each toe with her brush. Jeannie was so much cooler than the other side of any pillow!!!

Once they had both completed their preparations, they met in the middle, and I say that literally. I was lying there with nothing but wants, needs, and desires as they became involved in a savagely-serious tongue-sucking lip-lock. Their hands were traveling from tits to twat's with reckless abandon. They slowly made their way to the floor and began to exhibit their expertise with a sensually satisfying performance of a sticky-sixty-niner "(69)", announced by the sexy sounds of slurping up each other's love-nests. And once again they left me helpless. I had nothing to do except bust an occasional nut while watching them enthusiastically eating every possible body part that might be blessed with an opening or appear protrusive, including a professional performance of pussy-pruning preserved forever within **my mental museum of *art in afterglow*. *I love lesbians*!!! These two gorgeous young ladies have so lovingly taught me where to go, how to get there, what to do, and when to do it. They will always have a very special place in my heart and occupy a top listing in my world of Afterglow!!! Thank you, Jeannie, and your marvelous "RED SNAPPER", and your best friend, Kristi. I will love you all three forever!!!**

Sorry about that, I guess I got wrapped up in a memory. The world of Afterglow is a wonderful place to live when you are as old as I am and have lived the life I've lived!!! *(Try it, you'll like it)*

I don't suppose I have to give you blow-by-blow descriptions of what took place over the next couple of hours. But I will supply you with a few points of interest.

Once they were satisfied by each other's tongues an twats, they turned their attention to me. Lips were slurping, tongue slapping, armpit sucking, esophagus raping, sitting on my face, and sitting on each other's faces. Nipple and overlay tracing and biting, split-tail tummy-tipping, cock-sucking, ass-licking, kneecap-humping, shin-snatching, and toe-sucking. And then they untied me.

That is when the fun began!!! I was hotter than a firecracker on 4 July. They had me to the point where I was nut-busting constantly. It was almost like they had turned my prick into Jizzum fountain. I got my rocks sucking tits, toes, and twats. I licked armpits, eye-sockets, ears, ass-holes, clits, and the nape of their knees. I jerked off on both their breasts and massaged their titty's with my tongue. I raped both of their esophagus and flooded their flappers.

There were no holes barred and nothing was off-limits. Jeannie was sucking my cock. I was about to have an outpouring of appreciation so I pulled out and shot all over her nose and upper lip and up her nostrils. Kristi licked it off and sucked it out. They had taken me to an orgasmic level that if I thought one of them was going to touch any part of me, I would explode in a volcanic fashion of mother-loads.

Vaseline came on the scene and fingers were going where they didn't normally go. I wanted to fuck them both at the same time. I tried to strap on the double-sided dildo but my cock was in the way so I did one with each hand. Both their pussy's were extremely flexible with opening and closing. I could almost get my whole hand in them. Jeannie was sitting on my face and Kristi was sucking the head of my dick. They were both jerking the bottom part of my shaft up to meet Kristi's mouth. I stuck my thumb in Kristi's pussy and my middle finger in her ass-hole. I could feel them rubbing together as they met on the inside.

A **crazy, crazy, crazy** time; it was perfect for me at that time in my life. Jeannie and Kristi with a K and an I almost totally prepared me for things to come. All this happened and so much more during that one unbelievable lovemaking session when two totally uninhibited lesbians took me in and taught me everything they knew.

Over the next month to month and a half, I was their plaything and they were mine. We experimented with damn near everything. We were each other's toys. We had a menage a trois in Lafayette Park across from the White House. We had a menage a trois on the monument grounds and also at the edge of the reflection pool. We started to have one on the Capitol steps but the Capitol police broke it up.

What a great time. Too bad it had to end. But they say all good things even life must end. Life has been so good to me and love has been so good to me. Women have been extremely good to me and I have always tried to reciprocate although sometimes I failed. I know I have failed them more than they failed me.

If I should be so lucky as to have one or both of the two young ladies referred to in this portion of this book read it, I hope they can smile as they look back on that very special time for all of us.

Chapter 19
"Virginia Bound"

In the spring of 1964, I moved to Virginia and got a job at a local dry-cleaning plant in Annandale. I had responded to an ad in the paper for a delivery route man.

Part of my training program involved customer service at the front desk. The owners were somehow related; I think they were cousins. Both of them were very serious about their employees being well trained. Their training program was designed to make sure new employees were familiar with all phases of the laundry and dry cleaning process.

Route men were required to spend one week in the plant's main office where their training was overseen by one of the owners. More emphasis was put on the front desk and customer service than all of the other phases combined. Personality and people skills were looked at as priority plus.

This gave me the opportunity to become very well acquainted with all inner plant employees. It just so happened that female employees outnumbered the males 10 to 1. The only positions held by males were the pressers and cleaning machine operators. That was because those two positions were more dangerous.

In those days, female employees seemed to be somewhat protected. Possibly, they were even considered inferior as far as strength and durability was concerned.

Being as mentally unsure of myself as I was about the process of keeping other people's clothing clean, it didn't take me very long to show my eagerness to learn. By the end of my first day, I had achieved first name status with all employees present, including the pressers, cleaners, and one of the bosses.

I much preferred to fill my memory bank with information gathered from the front desk customer service and filing clerks. I noticed right away their willingness to make sure I was never alone while gathering information. They would somehow find a way to make it appear as though the party I was talking to at the time was not fully informing me of the questions I might have.

The one that tried the hardest to make sure I was receiving the proper training and correct information was Margie. Margie was 22 years old and had recently been promoted to assistant manager. She was the first one to teach me how to properly file the already pressed and packaged laundry or dry-cleaning pieces.

She also taught me how easy it was to lose my train of thought and get sidetracked or lost. Perhaps I should say, she made a special effort to teach me the ins and outs of filing clothing. Particularly, in the dresses, coats, and suit areas, I could have some privacy and not be seen by other employees.

This furthered my interest in how deeply embedded her desire for me to receive the best training possible really was. So I asked her if she would make herself available to enlighten me more, maybe for dinner that night. She agreed and gave me the name of a restaurant in the Seven Corners Shopping Center called the Inn of the Eight Immortals. She said it was a very good Chinese restaurant located close to where she lived and she would meet me there at 8 o'clock.

I hadn't realized it before but as it turned out, the restaurant was only a couple minutes from where I lived. If I had known, I would have walked. That would have been much easier than trying to find a parking place close to the restaurant.

I arrived in the parking lot of the restaurant right at 8 o'clock. There was a really long line waiting to get in. Apparently, it was a very popular restaurant. I drove by the front entrance a couple of times where the line started. I didn't see Margie, so I parked my car, walked up, and took my place at the back of the line. She had been waiting for me to arrive before getting in line. She must have been parked in a space where she would be able to view the line. I had just got in line when she came walking up.

We said our hellos and both started mumbling about the length of the line. Margie said, "I know this is a very popular restaurant but I have never seen the line this long. There must be something special going on or being served tonight." I came back with, "I would be surprised if we get waited on in an hour or so."

I asked her if she would like to try someplace else? She asked, "Where did you have in mind?" I replied, "Postonies is a nice Italian restaurant just on the other side of route 50 and up maybe a quarter of a mile toward the Beltway." She said, "That's fine, I like Italian food. I know where it's at so I'll follow you in my car."

As we were walking up to the entrance of Postonies, Margie said, "I think I'd like to have a drink or two before dinner. Let's stop by the bar first." I sure as hell didn't have a problem with that. I did kinda wonder why she wanted to drink herself into a conversation about work. I indicated it sounded good to me and said, "There's nothing like a drink before dinner to enhance the atmosphere. It sometimes clears the air."

We had a seat at the bar and she had a glass of house wine and I had a Schaeffer beer. We talked for a short time about her job, the business, and the owners.

I found out the owners were from North Carolina and they like to hire young ladies for the front desk reception area from North Carolina. She implied they thought the southern accent supplied a certain intrigue or welcoming to the customers.

Then she said, "There is also one thing you can be sure of. You will never see anything but beauty and good figures on the front reception line. The cousins are totally convinced that beauty sales."

She continued with, "The one cousin is so horny if you happen to step in front of him he insists on helping you set down. As soon as he touches you, his fly automatically unzips itself. I shit you not, and he's pretty damn fast, too. I was helping him close one night and he chased me all over the plant. I can tell you if and when he catches, whomever it may be, they will find out he is all hands and his mouth comes straight from France. But he's a helluva nice guy. I had been working for him for two weeks and been caught twice.

I wanted to buy a new car. He called the dealer up. I didn't even need a down payment. They had the papers ready for me to sign when I picked up the car. His other plus is he's really very loose with his money. He likes to have fun and doesn't want his wife to know about it. That makes it almost a safe situation. I don't mind if he expects a little more because I know the more he receives the more he is going to give me. I guess I'm funny that way—I kind of like nice things, and nice things tend to cost money. The next time, if there is a next time, maybe I'll cook dinner at my place, then you'll see how free and loose has helped me furnish my apartment."

I really didn't have a reply for her confession of sorts while spilling the beans on her boss. The only thing I could think of to say was, "Wow, sounds like a man after my heart. Yes, sir, I would have to salute him. I don't have a whole lot of money to be loose with but my love is free. However, I do not like to waste my energy running so if you run from me I'm not going to chase you. I have always felt there are better ways to spend my time and energy while having fun doing so. One of which is the best exercise for your heart known to man. It also gives you the opportunity to meet a lot of nice people. You can enjoy a little TLC and stay in shape. If one pursues that approach for exercise enough, they can build some damn good motor muscles, to say nothing of the long list of phone numbers one might acquire. However, that particular exercise might have some latent side effects, such as you probably will never get married. You may die alone but you will never be lonely. You can always keep the **memories of afterglow** burning by thinking of how much fun you had building all those muscles. Why in the hell are you telling me all this stuff anyway?" She replied, "I don't know, dammit. I guess I had a couple of drinks too many while I was preparing for the evening to begin. Either that or I didn't know why I accepted your invitation for dinner under the pretense of satisfying your desire to learn more about the job."

Margie just kept babbling, talking about nothing but letting me know when she gets nervous she also has diarrhea of the mouth. She went on with, "Other than the fact that I was attracted to you and I wanted to be with you. So let's talk business. I don't think you have anything to worry about. All the girls like you, the bosses like you, and you learn fast.

Now that we have discussed business, let's get down to business. I'm not really hungry. I think I'd rather have another drink and talk trash, how about you?" I replied, "Hey, sounds like a winner, let's get to it." I nodded to the bartender for another round apiece.

While we both had a pretty good idea of what the evening's outcome was going to be, I personally felt it would behoove me to pacify Margie in every way possible. After all, she was my boss. As an assistant manager, I didn't know if she had the authority to discharge me or not if she felt like it. I do know I felt I needed to respect her position.

I had made friends with three or four other young ladies that worked in the reception area. I would like to have somewhat of a mutual understanding of the situation between Margie and myself, especially if I were lucky enough to have an opportunity to go to dinner with one or all those lovely young ladies. I believe it would be nice to know Margie and I were on the same page if it comes to pass.

Margie likes loose money, free nice things, and me, I like pussy. There seems to be enough of everything to go around without anybody getting pissed off if we can agree ahead of time. Maybe that should be our trash-talking business arrangement of the evening. She seems to have had one too many to have anything to eat. Maybe I can convince her that she should consider being my main course, and dessert.

I stood up and said, "Margie, you seem to be a little edgy or nervous. I have to hit the restroom for a second or two. While I'm gone, why don't you slip into a seriously relaxed business arrangement state of mind? When I return you can decide whether you would like to continue our trash-talking here, or go somewhere we might be able to include some temptatious thoughts of comfort into our trash trending communiqués."

As I walked back to the bar and sat down, it was obvious Margie was deep in thought and quite possibly drowning at the bottom of her wine glass. Once I had reclaimed my seat, I reached over and gently touched her arm then whispered, "My dear, I think you should drink that thought. I will get you another drink with a new glass." As she looked at me, she reached over and emptied her glass in the drain on the other side of the bar.

I wasn't sure where her mind was, so I inquired, "What is your pleasure, Margie? Shall we stay here or go to my place or yours? You're the boss and it's your choice." She looked me straight in the eye without speaking for at least a minute. I could tell Margie was in deep deliberation of a decision. I thought she needed a little help so I smiled as I gave her arm a tender squeeze and mimicked her a kiss.

Without taking her eyes off mine, Margie responded with, "Make this one a margarita." I asked, "Would you like it with or without salt?" Our eyes were still locked together as she replied, "With please." I broke eye contact to order the drinks then turned to Margie and said, "You are aware salt is considered somewhat a product with qualities used for enticement or having similarities to aphrodisiacs. They say it warms the blood and heightens the senses." She broke her focus on my eyes smiled and said, "Good, maybe that's what we both need. Why don't you have some salt with your beer?" I responded with, "I've never tried it before so this is just for you." I put a touch of salt on my wrist, glanced over at Margie, then very slowly and sensually licked it off. As I touched my bottle to her glass for a toast, she smiled and said, "You have a very talented tongue. You managed that without dropping one salt granule." I came back with, "I just wanted to look good in front of my boss." She responded with, "It looked so good I can still feel it. And by the way, could we just put this boss business to bed." I anxiously jumped in with, "It sure sounds good to me." She retorted, "Okay, it came out wrong. It's a damn wonder I can talk at all after your talented tongue display. But let's get this shit straight while we're at it. I'll just shut my eyes and talk. I am the assistant manager of the plant where you work. I am not your boss. Furthermore, from my response to your short performance, I think I made it quite obvious I have no desire to be your boss. Bosses must show control. You have me at a disadvantage and I have absolutely no control. So let's have another drink before I push you off the barstool and insist you take advantage of me right here. And, Larry, you're sexy enough to look at and be around, so if you don't mind trying to save your sensual gestures for later when we are in a more suitable setting where you will be forced to follow through with them." I replied, "Yes, ma'am, I will certainly try. I can't say I didn't mean anything by it, but it must have surfaced with the thought of the salt."

Well, you've probably already guessed it, the rest of the night started right there. It began with her saying to me, "You know why I'm having such a hard time with this, don't you?" I just lifted my eyebrows and shrugged my shoulders. And she continued with, "Every damn one of those girls on the front desk talks about you like most men talk about a woman. They have mentally had you for lunch every day since you arrived on the scene.

I am the assistant manager. That provides me the luxury of their respect enough to allow me to enjoy my entitlements of being first." I inquired, "Being first for what?" She came back with, "Come on, Larry, don't act so damn naïve. I know you've heard the whispers. The whole crew would like to make you their hors d'oeuvre at a gang-banger party. Hell, Larry, you don't have a body part they have not already devoured in their minds.

Brenda and Gail wanted to be first but I won you with the rock-paper-scissors method. So you better damn sure make it worth my while because I'm going to get the 50 questions tomorrow. And if the whispers get too loud, my sugar daddy might go bankrupt. And I for sure as hell do not want that to happen."

I looked at Margie and said, "I don't have any idea what you are talking about. I never got the impression that's what was going on. I am simply there to do a job to the best of my ability. Although I know a lot of bosses mix business with pleasure. I'm not a boss, and I would find it very difficult to do the job I've been hired to do if I had to worry about what each employee was going to say when I smiled at another one or took one to lunch, especially since it's my first week on the job and I'm in training. I know it would surely interfere with my productivity to say nothing of my mental ability to learn what I needed to learn. And what it sounds to me like is you letting it interfere with your productivity. Why? I don't know. You are a beautiful girl. You have got the world by the ass and your boss by the balls. Play it out, girl, it's all working in your favor. Enjoy yourself as long as you can."

I continued with, "What do you say let's cut this bull-shit out and go somewhere to have fun. Oh, by the way, how does Brenda and Gail both think they can be first?" She smiled and said, "They are kind of like peanut butter jelly, or ice cream and cake. They do everything together, hell one can't go to the bathroom without the other. I'm sure you'll like it when it happens." I just smiled, shook my head, and didn't say anything.

Chapter 20
"Crocked and Cock Crazy"

Margie had inhaled five margaritas in about an hour and a half and was beginning to stagger-walk as we were on our way to the cars. I said to her, "Margie, why don't we leave your car here? We can take my car. There is a little parking problem at my place anyway." She looked at me with a question mark in her eye and said, "Okay, and how do I get back to my car?" I replied, "That's no problem. I only live a couple of blocks away and neither of us works until 2:00 tomorrow afternoon. I can drop you off here after breakfast."

She agreed to that and then said, "I don't work tomorrow, I took the day off. I didn't want to have to explain anything to the Boobzie-Twins while my "sugar-daddy" is around. I am sure it wouldn't take him very long to figure out that I had gone out with you. Since I don't like to be the focal point of friction at work. I thought it best to take the day off." I responded, "So you turn the focal point over to me? Thank you very much, my dear Margie. Since I was the last one hired, I should be pretty easy to fire."

She assured me that was not going to happen, that all I had to do is deliver a flirtatious-knockout-punch-line to either Brenda or Gail. Then she said, "It really don't matter which one because they have so much air in their head they will both fall for it. Then you become the boss. That will entitle you to a flavorful night of fun with that dynamic duo from Annandale named Brenda and Gail. Since tomorrow is Saturday and the weekend lies ahead, you might just have to force yourself to spend a little more time in bed. You think you can handle that, Larry?"

As much time as she had spent explaining all this to me about Brenda and Gail, it kind of made me wonder what she was doing out with me. We got to my place about 10:30 and she went right to work clarifying that very issue.

Margie took a couple of minutes in the bathroom to freshen up. On her way back, she found the bar, and just like she was at home, she fixed herself another margarita. She even found the container to dip her glass in for salt. I guess her hormones were starting to dictate where she would be going from there. I was fine with that because it was exactly where I wanted to go.

With her drink in one hand and unbuttoning her blouse with the other, Margie looked at me and said, "Where's the bedroom, Larry? I'm too damn young and happy with my present situation to get serious, so let's get this show on the road."

She was definitely born to be a supervisor. I thought to myself, I'm going to have fun with this. She seems to know exactly what she wants. I'm going to let her tell me what she likes, where to start, where to go, and what to do. But first I think I will pleasure myself by making this an exploratory project while preparing her personal properties.

I opened the bedroom door and turned the light on. By the time Margie got to the bed, she was halfway undressed. I said, "Hey, baby, maybe you should cut back on the salt a little bit. If you keep this fast pace up, you're going to be leaving before I get where you want me to go.

She looked at me started laughing and said, "Sorry about that, I guess I'm just so used to Mike being in a hurry. Most of the time, it is over before I get started." I replied, "Well, Margie baby, I'm not

Mike and I haven't had enough quickies in my life to know when to stop. I kinda like the "ole" hands on the clock to move slowly so I can remember where I've been and enjoy it later. Memories, my dear, of life, and love is what it's all about."

I motioned to the bed and told her, "Here, sit down and rest your feet and let me take your shoes off. As a matter of fact, just lay back and I'll take my time removing the rest of your clothes. Lovemaking is too much fun and way too important to have a hurry-up state of mind with. No matter how long it lasts, it's always over too soon."

I put a couple of pillows up against the headboard so she could lean back and prop herself up. Then I said, "Just let me know, darling, when you need another drink. I have a little prep work to do."

I loosened the catch and unzipped her skirt, then slowly helped it slide down over her thighs and legs. Margie then took her foot, and with a teasing-twirl, tossed it to the floor. Her blouse was open so I bent over and kiss-walked her tummy, up, down, and around until my tongue found her bellybutton.

From there my traveling tongue initiated a teasing trail of titillation to her twat. I kissed her pussy through her panties and pleasured her love nest with several soft lip-biting moves. Taking her panties between my teeth, I purposely included several pubic hairs to provide a tiny tilt of torture for her pussy pain sensation. Born to travel, my talented tongue took several trips on her love trail, presenting my ticket to ride to her belly button, tummy, and enter-thighs on each trip. I conducted a pubic hair pulling symphony on her still panty covered pussy. Margie insisted on helping me with my head maneuvers and mouth motion. She took my head in her hands and added the excitement to contact by turning the up, down, and around movements into a slow-rolling motion from the innermost part of one thigh to the other, pausing each time for me to provide more pleasurable pain from the lip-locking pubic hair pulling of her panty covered cunt. The hair-pulling pain seemed to be just what she needed to break through the numbness of tequila.

I performed a mouth to panty pubic hair pussy lip massage. Then I stiff-shaped my tongue to a point and slow-searched the surface of her panty covered pussy, hoping I would receive an invitation to enter from the slippery wetness that had been provided by the hunger of her secreting clitoris. I then tongue-tucked her panties to saturation by force-feeding them repeatedly into the warm, wet, and welcoming spread open lips of her pulsating pussy.

By this time my cock had achieved full firmness. Unable to resist the temptation of twat teasing, I unzipped my pants and put my pecker into tap-dance-mode on her tummy. Then I proceeded to take her blouse the rest of the way off. Once that was accomplished, I began to gently squeeze-pump her tits with her bra still in place. Margie took my hand and led my fingers directly to the valley of the dolls that separates the left from the right tit. This allowed me perfect access to the front hook release of her easy-off bra. As I unhooked her bra, I looked at her and said, "I had the feeling you were an uptown girl." Margie wore a sultry smile as she teasingly tongue-massaged the protrusive point of her upper lip. I had noticed that particular maneuver appears to be a commonly adopted practice for ladies who love sex.

Margie had started to unbutton my shirt. She hesitated a little, tipping her glass and finishing her drink while very sensually tongue washing the rim, making sure I saw it was free of salt. Then she handed her glass to me so I could prepare her another drink.

I fixed her another margarita with extra salt. While I was preparing her drink, she slipped out of her bra and panties. As I approach the bed, my prick was still outstretched through my zipper and Margie made it quite obvious she had something else in mind.

Sitting on the edge of the bed, she grabbed my cock, and with a fast four or five jerk-off motions pulled me closer, then swallowed the head of my prick. She began a fast hard suck-off procedure that provided a slap-snapping-sound as her sexy lips slid back and forth over the rim of my cock. Margie was applying such hard suction I had the feeling I was going to end up with a hickey on the head of my dick.

Holding her hand tightly around the base of my shaft, she finger trailed my main vein all the way up to the hole in the head of my prick that provides loves orgasmic over-flow. She began trying to force her tongue into that tiny opening as though she were going to tongue fuck my cock. Then she returned to that same fast hard suck-off process while all the time she was unsnapping my pants and unbuckling my belt. I, of course, am still standing there holding her drink.

My pants fell to the floor as I reached around with my other hand to the back of her head. I pulled her head towards my groin and began administering a rolling-mouth fuck. Margie opened her mouth wide as I force-fed her my entire cock-shaft. I could feel her chin rubbing against my nut sack as the head of my cock began to acquire a taste for her esophagus.

Chapter 21
"Riddin' That Train"

I squatted down a little and spread my thighs as I started cramming my balls into her mouth. Then I changed my mind, I knew there was a better way to accomplish this. I slowly backed my cock out of her mouth and through her desirably clinging lips.

Then I performed somewhat of a finger-drum-roll on her head and told her, "Here's your drink, honey, I'm going to finish getting undressed."

She immediately applied heavy suction on my shaft and tongue drained my main vein back and forth a couple of times. Then Margie pulled her tightly gripped mouth very fast over the head of my cock, which immediately surrendered a lip-slapping-pop along with the company of the cold-air shock to my sucked-off-hot-rosy-red-headed penis's exit.

By the time I got my shoes, socks, and pants off, Margie had finished her drink. With not a trace of salt left around the rim of her glass, she handed it back to me and asked, "Larry, would you fix me another drink, please?"

This must have been her seventh or eighth drink of the evening. I was beginning to get a little concerned about her. She wasn't that big. Maybe she weighed 110 or 115 pounds at the most. So I ask her, "Margie, are you sure you're okay? And do you really want another drink?" She replied with a very definite tone, "The answer is yes to both your questions, Larry. And before you asked me why, I will answer that question also. I am thoroughly convinced this is going to be such a wonderfully unforgettable evening. I am probably not going to want to remember it. I don't expect you to understand that, but I will promise you this, regardless of how the evening turns out or how inebriated I become, I will not interfere with your love life if you do not interfere with mine.

To you, memories are what it's all about, but to me, a memory can be a terrible interference. I'll be good to you if you will be good to me. That, however, does not mean that we are good for each other. But as you said earlier this evening, Larry, let's enjoy it while it lasts for it will all be over much too soon."

I returned to the bed to deliver her another drink, the same as the last one. She took it, never said thank you, fuck you, or go to hell. She drank it and teasingly traced her tongue around the rim of the glass a couple of times to secure the salt.

Not a word was said. We were both totally nude and knew exactly where we wanted to go. I had my always present and overwhelming desire for taking a ride on the E-Train. I'm not sure where it began, but I think it might have been spawned from the first really pleasurable act of sex I experienced when I was young. That would have been when Jeannie was my babysitter/sex instructor. She taught me to perform a finger-walking-massage procedure on each rib of her esophagus while she was giving me a blow-job. That-***"tender-touch-of-time"***- turned out to be the delivery moment of my very first coming/orgasmic explosion. I have no idea what happened. All I knew was I wanted it to keep happening and last forever. From that day forward, the esophagus became a dominant force in my mind for the inspiration of sexual needs.

(Back to the business at hand)

From what Margie said about Mike and her sex-capades, she must like swallowing cock-n-come. Neither of us saw any reason to waste time getting there, and we did not.

We both eagerly made our way to a good "ole" 69er. Margie quickly outmaneuvered me to occupy the top side. I believe it was because the top-side gave her a feeling of power. She would be able to control the depth my cock could achieve in her esophagus. The person desiring possession of the top side position of a 69'er usually feels a need for control. This way, Margie can also determine how fast she will allow my cock to reach a pleasurable depth.

I was pleasantly surprised to find that Margie was in a hurry to see just how far down into her esophagus she could force my cock without choking.

It could have been she was influenced by the alcohol. For whatever reason, it appeared she just could not wait to choke on my cock. Being the egotistical maniac that I am, I was happy to help her achieve her objective for self-induced cock strangulation by esophagus travel.

That achievement seemed to be considered a pat on the back, or a sign of a job well done. If nothing else, at least you knew you had a cock worthy of acknowledgment. And for some strange reason, when one has made the choices in life that I have, that becomes almost like a medal of honor.

Margie had made sure to make it obvious that she had no intention of doing anything that might be detrimental to the relationship she and Mike had. She appeared a little unhappy with certain aspects of their affair. But she knew with Mike she had the best of both worlds for someone her age. All she really had to do was satisfy his sexual desires when they surfaced. According to her, he never makes any other demands, and he does not mind paying for her sexual serving tray.

He apparently gives her everything she wants. I'm going to have to try to find out just how that works. If she wants a new car or more clothes, in what phase of a sexual rendezvous does she enter a conversation about wanting or needing something.

For example, she says he's always in a hurry so it cannot be worked out with a longer performance. It would have to be more intense or maybe even intrusive. Maybe it is at the end of a vacuum-packed main vein draining with that very sexy protruding point of her upper lip. The tender touch of prune possibly could rise a man's enthusiasm to pay extra. I could see someone with a lot of money paying extra for performances like that.

I read an article in one of the more popular sex magazines about people and the desires they were willing to pay extra to have satisfied. I also heard about this guy one time that paid a prostitute to blow up his ass-hole. That is a hard one for me to figure out. And I am someone who will let women do damn near anything they want to do to me. Why would he pay for it if it's going to happen as a normal response during sensual acts of sex? Who knows, maybe that's just all he wanted her to do. "No thanks, maam', no sex tonight, just blow up my ass-hole." Maybe she was blowing bubbles. I think that could be kind of interestingly cool.

My dad was always inventing different little gadgets. I'll bet he could've invented an ass-hole bubble-blower.

I have been trying to work my way back to the "E" train. No, I don't have a writer's block, I have a writer's cock. Margie did such a fucking fantastic job on that self-induced choking maneuver I'm still busy riding that same damn "E" train all these years later. Damn, she was good! She got it all in but the balls, and she's still gets my attention. I just gave her a 21-gun salute!!! My ears are your ears and I know what I want and need to hear. If you want to know the truth, I thought I'd give you a few minutes to put your mind back in gear and stop playing with yourselves. **"Ole" lady** five finger and little miss clit, and we all know if your nipples get hard when you suck your own tit; I'm your five fingers and your clit, I am the hardness of the nipples on your tit; We all need a break every now and then, So, break's over, all aboard, hop back in; Put it all aside, and get back to the ride; Hell, you already bought your ticket.

<u>(Now let's ride that "E" Train!!!)</u>

Chapter 22
"Esophagus Travel"

****(THE *** "E" *** TRAIN)****
*****COMMETH*****
here it
**KU-U-U-UMS!!!**

Margie made a couple forced deep throat dives into her tunnel of esophagus love with my cock. She had succeeded in building my ego by providing a few choking and gagging episodes. Then slowly returning to her sexual senses, she began to ride the chopping wave-like sensations provided by each rib-roll of her esophagus as it found its way over my prick's head. It reminded me somewhat of receiving a blow job on a passenger train. You experience the same choppy-waves as those large heavy steel wheels travel over each connecting rail joint.

The nice part about it was Margie was in total control of how the head of my cock and its rim would execute the approach to every rib of her esophagus. And she seemed never to be satisfied unless the results of the next rib became the intensifier rendering more depth with its sensational sexual pleasures than the last.

Margie knew exactly what she was doing. She also controlled the pressure applied to my main vein by the protrusion point of her upper lip. She gave my shaft a couple of minutes of a fast bumpy ride. I could feel her running interference with her tongue riding the top of my cock. She was forcing my main vein up hard against her upper lip for possible draining.

I began a nibble-nipping soft-squeeze clit-biting process. Margie lost it and immediately responded with hard suction on my cock from a fast mouth-fucking motion. She started moving her ass up, down, and side-ways trying to magnify the feelings of ecstasy my teeth and tongue were providing to her captivated clit. Margie announced exactly what she wanted and how it felt in several two-word exclamatory verbal disclosures of falling ecstasy: **"Oh-"God"!!!"-"Stop-Go!!!"-"Oh-Shit!!!"-"Don't-Stop!!!"-"Yes-Yes!!!"-"Oh-My!!!"-"Easy-Easy!!!"-"Go-Go!!!"-"Do-It!!!"-"Like-That!!!"-"Eat-Me!!!"-"Eat-Me!!!"-"Yes-Baby!!!"-"Go-Slow!!!"-"Do-It!!!"-"Do-It!!!"-"Now-Baby!!!"-"Now-Baby!!!"-"Oh-My!!!"-"Oh-Yes!!!"-"Eat-Me!!!"-"Eat-Me!!!"-"Yes-Yes!!!"** Suddenly, Margie changed position and put both hands behind my head and spread her legs as wide as she possibly could. Then she pulled my face hard into her vaginal parlor like she wanted a facial entry and was trying to smother me with secretions of her pussy's pleasure. For the finale, she whisper-grunted and cried, then screamed her way through one very long, what seemed like a never-ending, "Yeeeeeeeeeeeeeeeeeeeesss B-a-b-y, B-a-b-y, Oh my 'God', I have never felt anything like that before!" She started crying while at the same time continuing to hard-grind my face into her pussy and pelvic bone structure area, then added, "I just knew this night was going to be crazy. Larry, you are fantastic. How in the hell did you do that?"

We had both loosened our lust for additional sexual pleasures at the time and were laying there just kind of staying in touch with each other's bodies. Margie started weeping from the overwhelming feeling of ecstasy exposure she had just experienced. I very gently and consolingly slid my hand up one arm to her cheek and kissed her softly on the other shoulder as I made my way to her mouth. We both shared a tender moment. Then I said, "Margie my dear, what you received was a moment of tender orgasmic bliss of your own mental making. I only waited for you to tell me what you wanted and how you wanted it done. You are the miracle worker, my dear. Isn't making love magical and so much fun? I hope you never forget this night, I know I never shall." She looked at me with happy star-tears in her eyes. Happy star-tears speak with a very loud commanding voice. Her eyes sent me a clear invitation. I knew I had no choice except to both masterfully and magically secrete and eat my fill, forcing Margie's cup to overflow with a repeat performance and lasting memory of appreciation for a long-overdue lust-filled love-lava liaison.`

As our bodies reconnected, I reached up and smacked her hard several times on both ass cheeks. This resulted in her pussy and clitoris crushing my mouth, lips, teeth, tongue, and mind, serving up an abundance of her love sanctions for my reveling. She expressed herself with a pain-filled sound then thanked me with a short secretion squirt from her clit.

That's all it took. I knew the end results would be up to me from that point on. Women who like pain during sex normally do not like to inflict pain on their partners. They would rather respond positively to the pleasures they have received from pain inflicted.

I returned with a flurry of gentle left and right ass-cheek side-slaps causing her clitoris to slide softly across the tips of my teeth. I applied a very cordial tongue soothing massage to the tiny pinhole opening of her sexually explosive clit. Once it had achieved partial hardness, I slipped into a lip caress with a soft sucking kiss for orgasm enhancement. This happened almost immediately after each application.

Suddenly, I realized that she was riding my mouth and tongue so intently she had neglected my "E" TRAIN ride. Now she was sitting straight up on my mouth bouncing violently up, down, and around. Margie had flipped her orgasmic flow switch from part-time to full-time mode and was flooding my mouth and tonsils. I knew I had to make an adjustment and I had to make it fast. On her very next bounce upward, I slid the thumb of my right hand into her pussy and began a very aggressive hard and fast pounding thumb-fuck procedure on her cunt. While I was catching my breath, I was able to move just enough to align my mouth and tongue into a perfect position to play titillating tease games of torment with her little snow-white prune. With my thumb all the way inside her pussy to its bottom joint, I started caressing her tight twitching little butt-hole with my tongue. She started bouncing more and screaming louder while surrendering a creamy-dream stream of jizzum-juice all over my chin, shoulders, and upper chest. She reached her hand down to collect some of the runaway juices then grabbed my cock with both hands. Margie was double-handed squeeze jerking my prick so fast and hard it took about 10 seconds before I tried to shoot out the lights.

Realizing what happened, Margie's mouth immediately went south to engulf the head of my cock and bit down hard to let me know she was there. Then she continued to give an amazingly satisfying performance of cock-sucking. It was as though she was the only performer on stage at Carnegie Hall. Her lips were in rhythm with her tongue and she never missed a note while playing her heart out on my 8-inch skin-flute.

My juice producer started making me a little nervous with the short sharp pains it was sending through my nuts. It seemed like I had been providing Margie with a constant flow of short orgasmic shooters ever since I boarded the "E" train. In less than a second, she was fully mounted on my cock. Margie had left a dripping trail of her twat secretions from my chin down over my esophagus, chest, and stomach. Then she began some serious cock-hopping.

For about 30 seconds to maybe a minute, Margie administered some really rapid pussy pounding on my pecker. Each time, she received a climatic response from my cock she would raise her body off holding the head of my prick in her hand to ensure a perfect re-entry. Then she would slam her pussy down over my shaft almost engulfing my balls while screaming all the way down.

Her body weight forced the head of my prick hard against her inner pussy wall as though she was trying to punch another hole in it. This produced more screams of pleasurable pain from Margie. It also provided enticement for the "ole" jizzum-trail to overflow and once again my feelings of pride returned with flood status.

I'm not sure if it was just me thinking this, or if one of Margie's goals was to totally drain my reserve tank of come. But on the other hand, it seems like everyone I get involved in a lovemaking session with has that same goal. Maybe it's just my way of thinking. I thank "God" for granting me the youth and stamina to stay maybe at least halfway in touch with their reality.

Chapter 23
"The Virginator"

I was almost certain Margie had been missing out on one of most young ladies' favorite experimental acts while fulfilling their desires in the art of making love, being reasonably sure she was holding on to the prideful thought of virginity for her tight little snow-white ass-hole. I felt I must endeavor to do my best to make her enjoy her first experience with rear entry, or maybe even a little "DP." Hell, maybe I could teach her to do the backdoor boogie with a little double penetration. A little pecker and pinky seduction duet might be good for her attitude. It could give her *a-hole-different outreach to the art of lovemaking*.

I saturated my little finger with some extra juices that were just kind of lying around going to waste. As she started to go into that short fast rapid pussy pounding action on my cock, I made sure my pinky finger was well lubricated. Then I applied some of the escaping Kum-Jucies to her anal-opening and the area around it. I had a feeling that she knew what I was up to and maybe she wanted to try it; I know I did. Suddenly, the time was right, she was on lift-off about 10 inches above my dick using one hand as a pecker guide and waving the other one around as though she was riding a bucking bronco in a rodeo.

I continued to lubricate and massage the area around her anal opening. I was trying to make sure it was prepped for a painless easy entrance. In a flash, it happened. She was screaming as lockdown on my cock-pad was a success. My pinky had achieved full insertion into her ass-hole. I wasn't sure if she knew because the screams were all the same. Then suddenly, she said, "You dirty bastard, I don't even let Mike do that." I had succeeded in disturbing the petite status of Margie's pretty little prune by providing her with the pleasure of my pinky's presence.

She just kept right on force-feeding my cock as far into her vaginal cavity as it would go. Margie was seriously spreading the walls of her pussy from side to side while I covered them with a spray of love juices from my pulsating-pride-filled-prick.

My pinky finger was still celebrating the success of the new relationship it was sharing with her bashful butt-hole. Margie's cute little ass-hole got tighter and twitched with each tiny-rim-roll.

I reached my hand around to where her vaginal arteries were secreting a serious flow of orgasmic juices. The weep holes of her pussy walls showed signs that her appetite for sexual satisfaction had never happened like this before. It appeared as though Margie was attempting total submergence of my cock through the process of her salivating hungry-cunt.

I gave all my fingers an orgasmic lube job. Then I made mental preparation for her next lift-off and landing. This time, her sexy little butt-hole was being coveted by my middle finger.

Margie just kept on pressure pumping her pussy down over my shaft. All she said was, "Larry, you and I must talk about this later. But right now I am so full of ecstasy I just want to fuck you, suck your cock, and swallow all the kum you have to give me. I will say this, I know your finger is presently enjoying the prepping pleasures it's providing for my butt-hole. I do not, however, know why you decided to strip my only remaining orifice of its virgin status. But I do like the way you got there. You are very smooth and it feels kind of interesting riding up and down on your cock with that finger-fuck teasing-touch it provides through the inside wall of my ass-hole."

I have often wondered if or how women knew what all could be accomplish through positive power usage of that **split-open-hole** between their legs. Also, if a man knew how vulnerable he was from the lust-filled desirable pleasures presented to him by that same **split-tailed orifice.**

It has been going on since the beginning of time, so I suppose it was all made possible by design.

****Women are wonderful!****
(and)
****Men are morons!****

I have always approached my moronish-mannerisms bursting with pride.

(I'M YOUR MORON MARGIE!!!)

Chapter 24
"Margie's Moron"

Like clockwork, it happened. Or maybe I should say like cock-work it happened. This time Margie used a different approach to lift-off. She used a revolving 2 or 3 inch at a time jerk-off motion, with her pussy muscles tightening on my prick. Sometimes, she would revolve slowly all the way up and around then slowly back down my shaft, returning to the short strokes. She was trying to keep me in suspense of lift-off. I think she had a pretty good idea what might happen the next time her pussy swallowed my shaft.

While honing my moronish skills in an attempt to always do the best job possible, I continued to very liberally lubricate my middle finger with as much of Margie's pussy secretions as possible. I addressed the pleasures of keeping the area around my out of sight pinky very juiced up. This would ensure less pruning-pain if I had to perform a glancing-blow off the side of her butt-hole-rim's entrance.

Margie possessed the very best revolving rotation pussy jerk-off motion I have been subjected to in my life thus far. It was **so enjoyable** and orgasmically juicy. My prick must have felt like a little embryo swimming around in whatever an embryo swims in.

I lost track of what I should have been paying attention to until she was on her way back down my cock screaming, "Catch me if you can!" About the time I pulled my pinky out of Margie's prune. She slapped her ass down fast and forcefully. My middle finger was bent back almost flat against the back of my hand when she landed. I was sure she broke it. When I yelled, she knew something was wrong so she turned her head and looked back at me and said, "Well, for goodness sake, Larry, don't tell me you missed. I suppose we'll just have to try that one over again. Maybe we can get it right this time." Then she started those revolving cunt-elevator up my shaft jerk-off moves again. It must be feeling pretty good because she's having fun now and that's a good sign.

I had to work on my finger a little bit because it was bent and doubled back. I got it back and into position by the time she was ready to come back down. But then she stopped halfway down and went back up. This time she lifted her pussy lips all the way off the head of my prick. Then she dropped back down until her cunt swallowed my cock's head.

Margie was fucking with me. She knew what I had in mind and was trying to make it as hard on me as possible to achieve an easy entrance for middle finger dominance of her ass-hole. She used her guide hand to assist her revolving pussy in creating a sensational pussy-lip-lock-suction.

Margie had heavily sensitized the head of my pecker. I was having little jerky shocks shooting from side to side and around the rim on the head of my prick. It felt like 10,000 little jelly-fish-mother-fuckers was stinging my peckers' head at the same time, and with each sting came the feeling of having a mini-orgasm.

And wouldn't you know it, while I was thinking about how good the pain felt, Margie brought her ass down with a slam. I will say, she accepted it very well. Projecting a slight indication of possible discomfort, she smiled and asked, "How the hell did you manage that?" I replied, "Just my moronish luck, I guess. Did it cause you much pain?" She just looked at me and tightened the grip of her jerk-off and guide hand on my cock.

Margie continued revolving her pussy up and around my prick in a way that told me we would talk about it later. Suddenly, without warning, her cunt-lips left my cock standing hard and cold. She placed her ass-hole and pussy in position to be pleased by my tongue as she assumed the topside of a 69'er position and began sucking my cock.

If I had been informed of her desire for a (69'er), I might have been able to have kept my middle finger submerged snugly in her prune. I think that was part of Margie's plan for changing positions. She knew her ass-hole would no longer be playing the part of a pussy for a make-believe middle finger prick. That was something she hadn't been used to and she needed a little time to think about it. I was fine with that, besides it gave my finger a little time to get limbered-up and let the soreness go away.

I brought her love nest to rest on my chin and began a titillation treatment to her clit. Margie immediately began the same mouth and lips vacuum-cleaner-suction on the head of my cock. She accompanied it with the same slow hand jerking squeeze on my shaft. Her teeth were locked under the rim around the head of my prick. She was sucking so hard I am sure if I could have seen her face her jaws would have been caving in from the force applied through her savage suck-off session. She would suck up until the suction would spread and pull at the opening in the head of my penis then squeeze down, then she would squeeze up and suck down. Her teeth found the bottom of the rim around the head of my cock as her guide hand and her lips came together. Then Margie would start her suck and squeeze maneuvers all over again and repeat them time after time. My ass was bouncing around so much I couldn't believe she was able to keep the head of my cock in her mouth. The more my ass bounced, the harder her mouth and lips would clamp around the rim on the head of my penis. Then she doubled the strength of her suction.

The shocking sensation became so intense I knew I had to stop it. While bouncing and jerking about, as a result of her salacious sucking, I reached up with both hands and placed them on her shoulders. Then I immediately pulled down with as much strength as I could. At the same time, I forced my ass up to meet her guide hand as far as it would go. The suction was interrupted, and my prick's head, although I didn't like to admit it, felt so much better. Margie immediately started her vacuum-packed cock-sucking and squeeze-jerk-off process all over again.

I stopped her and said, "Margie, I need to see the head of my cock." She slap-suckingly-slurped her vacuum cleaner lips up over and away from the rim of my peckers' head. Once again, I was attacked by an additional 10,000 invisible little jellyfish mother-fuckers. I tried to come another hundred and fifty times. My nuts and whatever other come producing parts are involved were giving me nothing but excruciating pains of ecstasy.

I know they were trying to produce but I didn't feel any kum seeping out. I must have been empty. Then with a tight-lipped vacuum slurp-slapping sound, the attention being given to my love-stick was reduced to a slow massaging jerk-off motion. There it was, the head of my prick was bright red and about one third larger than it should've been. When Margie saw it, she looked at me. Her mouth flew open and she said, "Oh my "God", did I do that? Why didn't you stop me sooner?" I replied, "It seemed like you were having too much fun and I like it when you enjoy yourself. Besides, it was the first time I had ever been so savagely sucked-off and I was enjoying it also. Where did you learn that lip-lock suction and hand squeezing jerk-off motion would provide that kind of results?" She responded, "That's Mike's favorite thing. He taught me all the moves and how to squeeze in rhythm with the suck-off moves of my mouth, tongue, and lips. I guess I never took the time to look at the head of his cock. I will say it is much more fun and exciting when you are doing it because you want to instead of because you have to.

Most of our sex belongs to my mouth. We never fuck the normal way and we sure as hell don't make love. He's a nice guy. I know what he wants and he knows what I want.

My pussy was so hungry for a good cock-fucking. My mind and body were aching for the excruciatingly painful feelings of ecstasy you made happen for me. I have enjoyed sharing those feelings with you, Larry. Through our performances of orgasmic bliss, I have enjoyed more painfully tender, tantalizingly, tormenting tricks of the lovemaking trade in one night than I could ever hope to experience with Mike in a lifetime.

I thank you very much for that, Larry. So much so I almost feel like I should pay for your pleasuring performances. I can only hope it happens again. If it does, it has to be with no strings attached, and oh, by the way, don't ever expect this confession to happen again. All I will ask of you, Larry, is, just perform, baby, and I will do the same."

I asked her, "Did he tell you it felt good and he liked it?" She came back with, "Oh, yes, that's one of his stipulations. Just before he leaves, he has to have a few minutes of hard penis-head-sucking and cock-squeezing action." I said, "Damn, Mike must have some desires that tend to support masochism.

Chapter 25
"Her Icy Box"
(or)
"The Ice Man Cometh"

I didn't want to use up all the ice that I kept in my bar so I went to the kitchen, got a bowl, and emptied a couple of trays of ice cubes into it. Then I returned to the bedroom for a little help in solving my enlarged red-headed pecker problem.

Margie seemed to be truly disturbed over the possibility that she and her vacuum cleaner cock-sucker-mouth had caused me discomfort. So much so that as I returned with a bowl full of ice, she took it out of my hands, then said, "Larry, I am so sorry... I didn't realize what was happening. Lay down, baby, and prop your ass up with a pillow. I will try to calm down what I sucked up."

I wasn't sure what she had in mind but I soon found out. The pillow lifted my ass up off the bed far enough she could put the bowl under my nut sack. Then she started a very interesting procedure of cooling to comfort the head of my cock.

Margie had gone to the bathroom and brought back a couple of large towels and a hand towel. She placed one of the towels under the bowl of ice, then she took my cock in one hand and bent over to kiss and make it better. She began a soft-loose-wet-lipped massage while totally covering her other hand with ice. Once the palm of her hand got cool, she picked up two ice cubes, put one in her mouth, and placed the other one at the base of my shaft. It slowly began to melt and drain down around each side of my ball bag.

Margie took the hand she had iced down and placed it very gently on my pricks head. She picked up the ice cube from the base of my love-stick and began to slide it up and down then around the lower half of my shaft.

This was all beginning to feel very nice. Because of the way she was responding, it made me start to wonder if this evening might become endless. That was okay with me. I had become quite fond of never-ending lovemaking sessions.

The shooting shockers had started to subside and had become nowhere near as painful. Margie once again put her lips and mouth over the head of my penis. This time, the inside of her mouth was very cool from the melted ice cube. She got two more ice cubes and repeated the procedure on the lower half of my shaft, then she let another one partially melt in her mouth. She kiss-caressed the head of my cock with tender loving care from her icy-tongue massage.

While this process was taking place, she started a rolling cool hand treatment on my balls and groin area. Then once again, she visited the head of my prick with a cool mouth and lips along with a partially melted ice cube. She succeeded in tongue rolling it around the rim and on top of the head of my cock. This was part of her continuous care treatment for my swollen red-headed pecker.

This time, when she relinquished control of big-red, she provided a slobbering kiss-roll followed by a true to life blow-job. Margie was really trying hard to undo what she had done and keep me erect during the process. After repeating the same performance four or five times, things were getting back to normal. I was thinking about continuing our lovemaking session. I didn't know whether I could produce anymore kum, but I knew I was willing to try.

Margie must've been thinking the same way because the next thing I know she stuck an ice cube up my ass. I jerked a little from the shock but it didn't hurt. It made me forget about the pecker pain, but damn it was getting cold in there.

I looked up at her and she was laughing as she said to me, "How'd you like that, baby? Pay-back is hell, isn't it?" I grabbed her, pulled her down on the bed, and got a handful of ice. I spilled the rest of it all over the bed along with the water that had melted, then said, "So you want to play like that, do you?" I partially laid across her stomach and held her legs down with my leg while I packed her pussy and her ass-hole full of ice.

The bed was wet from the ice water I had spilled and becoming more-so from the melting ice. I didn't give a shit. What are beds for except to have fun on? And that's what we did for the next hour, rolled around on a wet bed with ice cubes and had fun.

After having filled her vaginal canal and anal cavity with ice cubes, I thought it might be a good idea if I tried to get them out. Otherwise, she may become frigid and never want to fuck again. I was hoping that wouldn't happen because I was ready to start all over.

I slid down and put my mouth to her pussy and tickled her clit then started sucking. That didn't work. I had to go in with my fingers and persuade the ice cubes to exit her icy-box. Margie was a good sport about it all, but she let me know that her **split-tail** was freezing and hurriedly helped me succeed in unpacking her pussy as well as her frost-bitten-butt-hole. Once we had accomplished that, it was on.

We slipped immediately into that good "Ole" Taurus favorite(69'er). Together, we ate pussy and sucked cock, licked ass-holes, and butt-fucked for the next 30 or 45 minutes. Then we passed out on a wet bed.

I woke up stiff and wet, told Margie goodnight, and went to the couch. In a few minutes, she followed me. I got up and got a dry cover then we went to sleep cuddling on the couch.

Over the next few months, I enjoyed all the pleasures of pussy and lovemaking that fantastic front line of females could provide me with. I wish I could continue this bedtime story by describing those next few month's activities **Blow-by-Blow**. I am afraid that will have to wait for my next book. I mean, after all, I can't put everything in one book. And I think if you would tell me the truth you probably need a little time to recuperate.

You do know the four worst places in the male body to get a cramp, don't you? That would be your tongue, your cock, and your nut sack, and of course, our favorite little miss five finger. Now for the **split-tails,** (or) if you prefer the **young ladies,** I would have to guess their jaws, their tongue, their tits, their lower torso tummy area, their twats, and of course, those talented toes. They have so many more beautiful body parts to worry about than we do.

So, out of respect for those gorgeous hunks of female flesh, rest up and be prepared for our next bedtime story. Until then, this is your friendly bedtime storyteller, Pat Parsons, wishing you all many happy hard-ons and pulsating-pussy's.

Good night to you from our ice-cold tongues and cuddly couch. Oh, yes, and Margie's now very warm pussy-lips!!

The best is yet to KU-U-U-M!!!

PAT
PARSONS

Pats thoughts

The book introduction for **Split-tales** of **Split-tails,** much the same as the forward, can be and was written by another party.

Portraying his familiarity with my outlook on life and love, along with my zestful zeal for life. He willingly infringed upon his memory of an almost life-long friendship. A friendship that had sometimes elevated him to participant status and he became the recipient of special pleasures during several events throughout my life and our acquaintance.

Using knowledge acquired he tried to prepare future readers for my unusually special and wonderfully blessed life. I hope, through his efforts, you will have found the introduction much more relaxing on your mind, eyes, and heart. Or if you are a person who enjoys reading out loud such as I sometimes do, I would also include your lips, and ears.

Showing my appreciation with words of rhyme for each and every one of the ladies in my wonderful love filled life, was the easiest and the very least I could do. Oh, how they taught my love to grow, they made my eyes and my heart overflow; as they claimed their place and filled, my wonderful world of *AFTERGLOW*: I wanted to thank them in every way possible for being there for me. It is also something I felt the deep desire to do. As the years have come and gone there is very little else I could do for them.

Unless of course, they all got together and forced themselves on me. Then I suppose I would just naturally have to die happy. What a dream that would be. As you have probably already noticed, I love to dream.

It is my sincere wishes, through the use of many casual clichés and moronish mannerisms, with lines of alliterative measures rendering pleasures of metamorphosis status, along with a few lines of poetry, I have embodied your favorite pleasure seeking pass time with a satisfactory level of literary content. My only regret would be, I know there is no way you could enjoy reading it half as much as I enjoyed living it.

Sincerely,
Pat Parsons

**Unconscious midnight mumbling
from my world of**

"Afterglow"

hyperbole, yes hyperbole – is a word, dumb ass
you will find the meaning in the looking glass
if you see yourself and hold your place
the end of an era you will erase
if you choose to look into the deep
it tells not the time of life that's cheap
oh, the lack of luster one must feel
when genius trumps what's really real
when all life's pleasures are at large
is there no excitement to your charge
denial must be, cry me to sleep
if all that's left, is for you to weep
from here to for and nothing more
gives life one option, shut the door!!!
But then, your genius does explode
into a verbiage mother-load
and once again you can proclaim
there is no fire without a flame
that flame that never sets me free
the flame that burns inside of me
the flame that fires my heart and soul
the flame that never lets me go
'tis there, it's there no matter where
once more, to go from here to there
without a question of but where!!!
who knows where it is all going

do you know what you are doing
if I thought for one minute that I knew
do you think I'd do the things I do
one serves life as a peasant slave
to wish for things they cannot have
watching others that have flourished
feeling motherless, unloved, unnourished
though contradiction fills the air
it may be time I should declare
the one that holds the heart and soul
is the one that truly has control
and I will happily confess
'tis the one that I love best
she sure gave my heart a whirl
she was my world, she was my girl
from then and now to afterlife
she was my wife, she was my wife!!!

****

The midnight mumbler never sleeps
his whole existence is to weep
and search for memories that grow
all through his world of *"afterglow"*

("MKV")

About The Author

I was born in a small town in southern Virginia near the Tennessee border. When I graduated from high school, I got a job. I got in trouble several times, mostly from partaking of the forbidden fruit. Barely managing to not get shot or go to jail, I decided I would be better off living in the more densely populated area and moved to a larger city.

Staying true to the theme of my heart and mind's desires, I achieved my objective in learning what I needed to know. I did so by trying any and all possible acts of sex ladies could subject me to and didn't have to look over my shoulder in the process. As a result, my sexual escapades or rendezvous are mounted in number. They became written memoirs or tapes to be used in the processing of this particular book and others.

My hope is to enlighten my literary audience as to how much happiness can be found in life if one works hard at doing things for not only self-satisfaction but the satisfaction of others as well.

(Or maybe I just wanted everyone to know how much fun can be found in "loves-lustful-lap" of afterglow!!!) Now my home is right where I belong. Yes, my mind and my heart has taken up permanent residence in the same place they spent the majority of their life. I relish and dwell with the afterglow of memories in the mid to lower abdomen area of all the ladies that have worked miracles for me!!!